Mel Bay Presents

UP THE NECK

By Janet Davis

CD CONTENTS*

DISC-1

1. Tuning [:45]
2. Bluegrass Roll Patterns (pg. 8) [:53]
3. The Forward Roll Pattern (pg. 9) [1:12]
4. The Mixed Roll Pattern (pg. 10) [:52]
5. The Forward-Reverse Roll (pg. 11) [:46]
6. The Backward Roll (pg. 12) [1:08]
7. Bile 'Em Cabbage Down (pg. 13) [:37]
8. Forward Roll (pg. 13) [:52]
9. Backward Roll (pg. 14) [:36]
10. Forward-Reverse Roll (pg. 14) [1:07]
11. Salty Dog Blues (pg. 15) [1:18]
12. Backward/Alt. Forward Roll (pg. 15) [:54]
13. The Standard Chord Patterns (pg. 19) [1:13]
14. F-Position Pattern (pg. 19) [:55]
15. D-Position Pattern (pg. 20) [:49]
16. Barre-Position Pattern (pg. 20) [:46]
17. E-Minor Chord Pattern (pg. 21) [1:05]
18. Cumberland Gap (pg. 22) [1:43]
19. Alternate Part B (pg. 22) [:52]
20. Train 45 (pg. 23) [1:09]
21. John Hardy (pg. 24) [:30]
22. Alternate Forward Roll (pg. 25) [1:03]
23. Variation (pg. 26) [1:16]
24. Little Maggie (pg. 27) [:51]
25. Up-the-neck Arrangement (pg. 27) [:40]
26. 1st Arrangement (pg. 28) [:46]
27. 2nd Arrangement (pg. 28) [:37]
28. 3rd Arrangement (pg. 28) [:45]
29. Don't Let the Deal Go Down (pg. 29) [1:16]
30. Variation #2 (pg. 30) [:37]
31. Variation #3 (pg. 30) [:39]
32. Wildwood Flower (pg. 31) [1:14]
33. The House of the Rising Sun (pg. 32) [1:05]
34. Basic Up-the-Neck Licks (pg. 35) [1:15]
35. Lick #3, #4, #5, & #6 (pg. 36) [:52]
36. Train 45 (pg. 37) [1:13]
37. Little Maggie (pg. 37) [:47]
38. John Hardy (pg. 38) [1:28]
39. Mama Don't Allow (pg. 39) [1:06]
40. Crying Holy Unto the Lord (pg. 40) [1:21]
41. The "Identity Factor" (pg. 41) [:35]
42. Chord Progression #1 (pg. 42) [:55]
43. Chord Progression #2 (pg. 42) [:45]
44. Chord Progression #3 (pg. 43) [1:09]
45. Lonesome Road Blues (pg. 44) [:49]
46. Substitute Licks (pg. 44) [:31]
47. Roll in My Sweet Baby's Arms (pg. 45) [1:10]
48. Variation #2 (pg. 46) [1:03]
49. Pick-up Notes (pg. 47) [1:18]
50. G Licks (pg. 48) [1:52]
51. C Licks (pg. 49) [2:14]
52. D Licks – 1st-4th lines (pg. 50) [:52]
53. D Licks – 5th-8th lines (pg. 50) [1:17]
54. A Licks (pg. 51) [:58]
55. F Licks (pg. 51) [:56]
56. E Licks (pg. 52) [1:01]
57. B Licks (pg. 52) [:59]
58. B-flat Licks (pg. 53) [:53]
59. F-sharp Licks (pg. 53) [:28]
60. Am Licks (pg. 54) [:48]
61. Bm Licks (pg. 54) [:30]
62. Cm Licks (pg. 54) [:26]
63. Em Licks (pg. 55) [:41]
64. Dm Licks (pg. 55) [:37]

DISC-2

1. Chord Progression #1 (pg. 56) [:51]
2. Alternate Licks (pg. 56) [:31]
3. Chord Progression #2 (pg. 57) [:36]
4. Chord Progression #3 (pg. 58) [:34]
5. Lonesome Road Blues (pg. 59) [:49]
6. Substitute (Alt.) Lick (pg. 59) [:26]
7. Variation #2 (pg. 60) [:59]
8. Little Maggie (pg. 61) [:26]
9. Substitute Licks (pg. 61) [:28]
10. Salty Dog Blues (pg. 62) [:34]
11. Variation #2 (pg. 62) [:32]
12. Roll in My Sweet Baby's Arms (pg. 63) [:45]
13. Alternate Licks (pg. 63) [:43]
14. Jesse James (pg. 64) [1:51]
15. Harmony Notes (pg. 67) [:23]
16. Worried Man Blues (pg. 69) [:22]
17. Forward Roll Pattern (pg. 70) [:53]
18. Chord Positions (pg. 71) [:59]
19. Other Roll Patterns (pg. 72) [:57]
20. Substitute Licks (pg. 73) [:57]
21. Red River Valley (pg. 74) [:20]
22. Variation #1 (pg. 75) [:54]
23. Variation #2 (pg. 76) [1:00]
24. Hand Me Down My Walking Cane (pg. 77) [:20]
25. Forward Roll Pattern (pg. 78) [:54]
26. Substitute Licks (pg. 79) [:56]
27. Wreck of the Old 97 (pg. 80) [:19]
28. Alternate Forward Roll (pg. 81) [:52]
29. Variation #2 (pg. 82) [:54]
30. Variation #3 (pg. 83) [:37]
31. The Ending [:30]
32. Connecting Links
    Up and Down the Neck (pg. 86) [:35]
33. Lost Indian (pg. 87) [1:33]
34. Sitting on Top of the World (pg. 88) [:47]
35. Variation #2 (pg. 89) [:47]
36. Altered Roll Patterns (pg. 90)
    & Black Blossom (pg. 91) [1:16]
37. Wildwood Flower (pg. 92) [:54]
38. Variation #2 (pg. 92) [:52]
39. Sally Goodin' (pg. 93) [:50]
40. Variation #2 (pg. 93) [:30]
41. Variation #3 (pg. 93) [:37]
42. Sally Ann (pg. 95) [:51]
43. Variation #2 (pg. 96) [:49]
44. Don't Let the Deal Go Down (pg. 97) [:24]
45. Variation #2 (pg. 97) [:22]
46. Variation #3 (pg. 97) [:22]
47. Look Down, Look Down (pg. 98) [:56]
48. Variation #2 (pg. 99) [1:03]
49. Melodic Licks (pg. 100) [1:08]
50. Dixie (pg. 101) [1:36]
51. Cuckoo's Nest (pg. 102) [:44]
52. Crazy Creek (pg. 103) [1:24]
53. Limerock (pg. 104) [2:35]
54. Gray Eagle (pg. 107-109) [1:51]
55. Using Chromatic Licks (pg. 110) [:45]
56. Hamilton County Breakdown (pg. 111) [:35]
57. Variation #2 (pg. 111) [:33]
58. Variation #3 (pg. 112) [:33]
59. Cumberland Gap (pg. 113) [1:17]
60. Variation #2 (pg. 113) [:25]
61. Lonesome Road Blues (pg. 114) [:18]
62. Working on a Building (pg. 115) [:24]
63. Variation #2 (pg. 116) [:20]
64. Salt River (pg. 117) [:49]
65. Moveable Licks (pg. 119) [:32]
66. F-Position Licks (pg. 119) [:36]
67. F-Position Licks Continued (pg. 120) [:39]
68. Barre-Position Licks (pg. 120) [:22]
69. She'll Be Coming Around the Mountain (pg. 121) [:41]
70. Dill Pickle Rag (pg. 122) [:45]
71. Black and White Rag (pg. 124) [:51]
72. Salty Dog Blues (pg. 126) [:29]
73. Salt River (pg. 127) [:40]
74. Part B (pg. 128) [:32]
75. Using Back-up Licks (pg. 129) [:19]
76. 12-Bar Blues (pg. 130) [:31]
77. Hear Jerusalem Moan (pg. 131) [:40]
78. I Don't Love Nobody (pg. 133) [:55]
79. Endings-Group 1 (pg. 135) [:39]
80. Endings Continued (pg. 136) [:31]
81. Group II (pg. 137) [:34]

A recording and video of the music in this book are now available. The publisher strongly recommends the use of these resources along with the text to insure accuracy of interpretation and ease in learning.

Cover photo courtesy of Liberty Banjo Company, Bridgeport, Connecticut.

1 2 3 4 5 6 7 8 9 0

Visit us on the Web at www.melbay.com — E-mail us at email@melbay.com

CONTENTS

FOREWORD

"Up the neck" of the banjo involves playing between the 5th and the 22nd frets of the fingerboard.* This book is intended to provide you with the basic principles and techniques for developing the ability to play any song in the three-finger style of playing in the up-the-neck area of the banjo.

People often find it difficult to read the double-digit numbers involved in playing up the neck. However, just as it was difficult to read tablature for the first time, you will find that you will see the same numbers over and over, and you will begin to recognize the same patterns up the neck, just as you do when playing down the neck. Because these are related to chord positions, it will help to concentrate on the numbers involved with playing each chord, particularly the G, C, and D chords from which the left hand will work. These will become familiar to you within a very short time, and will be easy to relate to the fingerboard.*

This book is divided into chapters, with each chapter building upon the information presented in the previous one. The songs presented in each section demonstrate the particular technique(s) discussed in that chapter. However, the songs are also intended as playable arrangements. The more you play up the neck using these techniques, the easier it will be to develop your own arrangements using these techniques.

I have used these techniques for many years with my banjo students, and they seem to have worked well. I hope they will work well for you, also.

Happy Pickin'!

Janet Davis

Janet Davis

---

*NOTES_____

1. Throughout this book, the term "higher" will refer to higher in pitch or in fret number.
2. This book assumes that you have had some experience with tablature and with playing the banjo. You do not have to be an advanced player, however, to learn to play up the neck. Basically, this book begins with the upper beginning level and works through the techniques into the advanced level.

INTRODUCTION

The three-finger style of playing was popularized in the early 1940s primarily by Earl Scruggs and Don Reno, and has continued to be one of the foremost styles for playing the five-string banjo. In this style of playing, the melody notes for a song are surrounded by background notes, which are determined by the chords to the song. Patterns are involved in playing up the neck, just as they are involved with playing on the deeper tones of the banjo. Many of the *same* patterns (rolls and licks) can be used in many different songs for the same chord. As you begin to work with these patterns in songs and learn how they are used, the fact that they are played in the up-the-neck area will begin to seem natural. In fact, you should find it fairly easy to begin working out your own up-the-neck arrangements fairly early in the book.

As this book progresses, you will learn how to connect up-the-neck and down-the-neck licks smoothly, how to switch a lick for a lick for single chords, how to create variations, incorporate the melody, etc. The final sections of this book involve techniques developed by Bill Keith, Bela Fleck, Scott Vestal, and other influential banjo players of the 1990s. It is important to realize that the techniques which are used in the advanced sections are developed from the techniques covered in the earlier sections of the book. Therefore, it is important to understand the basics, first.

UP-THE-NECK ARRANGEMENTS

It will help to realize that *up-the-neck arrangements are often played as second variations* and, therefore, there is more freedom to deviate from the basic melody. (The first arrangement usually establishes the melody in the mind of the listener, so that he or she can appreciate the various techniques employed as the basic tune is expanded upon in subsequent variations.)

Up-the-neck arrangements are frequently of two basic types:

1. *An arrangement with a strong sense of melody.* This type of arrangement is generally based upon the **standard roll patterns,** where one finger of the right hand is used to pick the melody notes, while the other two right-hand fingers play background notes based upon the chords to the song. **Licks** are often used as fill, rather than as the basis for this type of arrangement. Songs which have words often fall within this category.

2. *An arrangement which deviates from the basic melody.* This type of arrangement is comprised primarily of **licks** (patterns or motifs). Arrangements which are comprised primarily of licks can be absolutely void of the tune for the song and still work, as long as the licks are played for the correct chords to the song. Generally, these songs will have a specific motif which will serve as the identifying factor for a listener, such as the intro to "Bugle Call Rag." Breakdowns usually fall within this category.

The following chapters of this book will take you through the development of arrangements which fall within Type I and Type II, as well as arrangements which use a combination of these techniques.

THE Y POSITION
RIGHT-HAND PLACEMENT

When playing up the neck of the banjo, using the higher fret numbers, the right hand should be positioned *near the fingerboard* (very close to the 22nd fret), and *not by the bridge.* This is usually referred to as the *Y position* on the banjo head. The banjo will have a mellower tone when the right hand picks the strings from this position. In other words, in the Y position, you pick the strings close to the neck of the banjo, rather than by the bridge.

When returning to the deeper tones (open string through 5th-fret area), the right hand should return to the area by the bridge in order to achieve a brighter sound. This is usually referred to as the *X position.*

In this manner, you can work with the overall expression of the song. As you become more skilled at working with the different right-hand positions on the head of the banjo, you may find from time to time that, even though you are playing up the neck, you prefer to play near the bridge until you come to a specific passage in a song so that you can *then* move to the Y position in order to enhance the effect of that passage. However, **when first working up the neck, place your right hand next to the fingerboard at all times.** Note: This may be a conscious effort at first, but eventually this will become automatic.

RIGHT-HAND POSITION

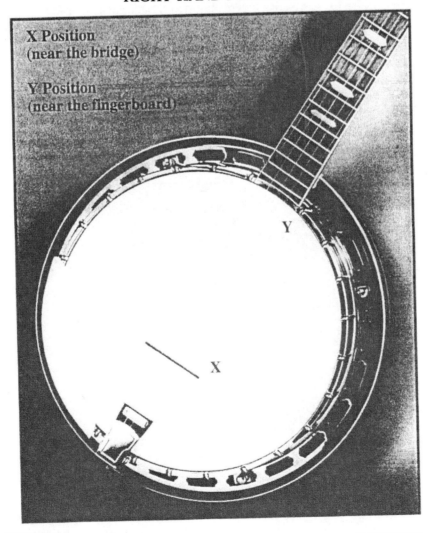

*NOTES
1. See page 85 for advanced techniques concerning the X and Y positions.

7

BLUEGRASS
ROLL PATTERNS

There are *four standard roll patterns* which can be used as the basic foundation for any arrangement of any song, when the arrangement is played up the neck of the banjo in the bluegrass style of playing. These are:

    1. **Forward Roll:** I M T I M T I M (right-hand fingers).
    2. **Mixed Roll:** T I T M T I T M.
    3. **Backward Roll:** M I T M I T M I.
    4. **Forward-Reverse:** T I M T M I T M.

It is important to realize that:

    1. Each pattern is a right-hand picking pattern.
    2. Each pattern consists of eight notes of equal duration.
    3. Each roll pattern also has an *alternate* pattern, which is frequently used to play up the neck of the banjo.

It is important to become familiar with the standard roll patterns for several reasons:

    1. You can always fall back on a roll pattern when you don't know what to play. It is always safe to play a roll pattern when you are improvising, even if you have never heard the song before. You can simply play the chords to the song with the left hand and play the same pattern over and over with the right hand for an entire song, and you will have an arrangement that will work. (Your arrangement will have a "bluegrass sound.")

    2. A complete song can be worked out in the up-the-neck area of the banjo, including the tune for the song, by playing only one standard roll pattern for every measure of the song, and by incorporating the melody for the song into the roll pattern, throughout the entirety of the song. (This will be demonstrated in the section on steps for arranging, page 66.)

    3. The melody for a song can easily be incorporated into the roll patterns by playing each melody note with the same right-hand finger each time that finger occurs in the pattern. Generally, the finger that begins the roll pattern will be the finger that picks the melody to the song, while the other two fingers play background notes based upon the chords being held with the left hand. (You may have to alter the rhythm of the melody somewhat in order to fit the roll pattern you are using. This will be covered in detail later in this book.)

    4. Licks are built from roll patterns. Identifying the right-hand pattern will help you learn the lick. (If you hear a new lick and can identify the right-hand pattern it is using, it should be easier to figure out how to play the lick.)

ROLL PATTERN
(USING THE FORWARD ROLL):

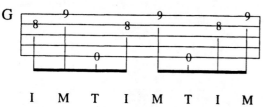

    I   M   T   I   M   T   I   M

LICK
(USING THE FORWARD ROLL):

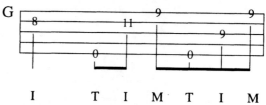

    I   T   I   M   T   I   M

    Note: Each of the above items is covered in detail in this book. However, it is important to first familiarize yourself with each of the rolls by name *and their alternate patterns.*

THE STANDARD
ROLL PATTERNS

These patterns are the building blocks for playing songs on the banjo, both down and up the neck. The alternate patterns are as important as the basic rolls when playing up the neck.

1. THE FORWARD ROLL PATTERN

The *forward roll* pattern adds drive to a song and therefore is one of the primary rolls used in the bluegrass style of playing. Although the index finger begins the pattern in the following examples, any of the three right-hand fingers can begin the roll. The pattern is determined by the order or sequence in which the right-hand fingers follow one another.

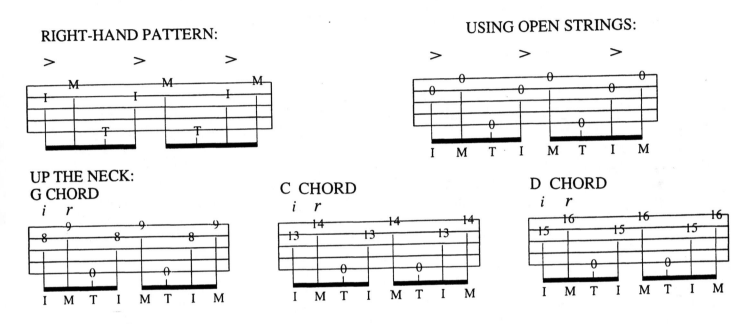

1A. THE ALTERNATE FORWARD ROLL

The *alternate* forward roll pattern is a variation of the forward roll (above). This pattern is commonly used to play up-the-neck arrangements. Notice, also, that this right-hand pattern is the same one that is used to begin "Foggy Mountain Breakdown." The third note can be picked with the thumb or the index finger (your choice).

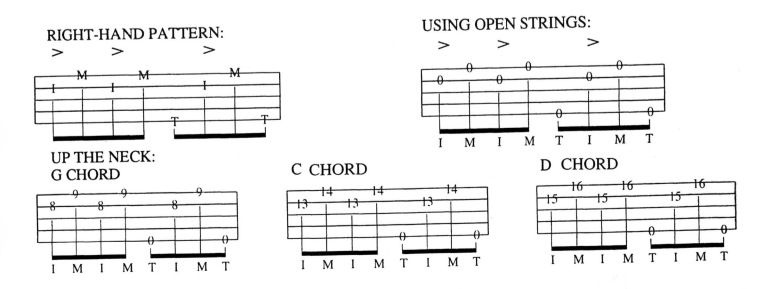

2. THE MIXED ROLL PATTERN (ALTERNATING THUMB)

The *mixed roll* pattern is effective for songs played at any tempo. Every other note should be accented when playing this pattern, with extra emphasis on the first and the fifth notes. Notice the back-and-forth feeling of this pattern; it is often used to provide a rocking effect, rather than drive.

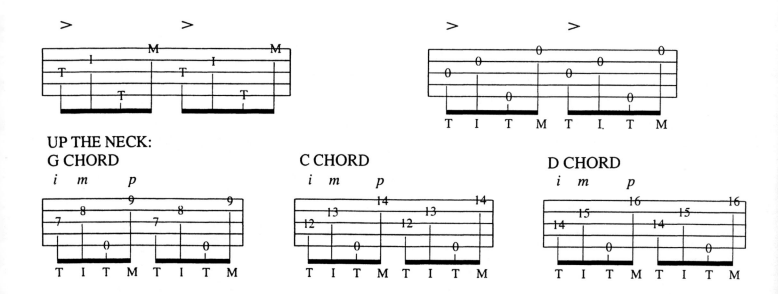

2A. THE ALTERNATE MIXED ROLL

The *alternate* pattern plays every other note with the middle finger of the right hand, rather than the thumb. There are several possible and very effective variations on this roll pattern. Experiment by beginning the pattern with the right index finger, using this finger to play every other note. The finger that begins the pattern generally picks the melody notes.

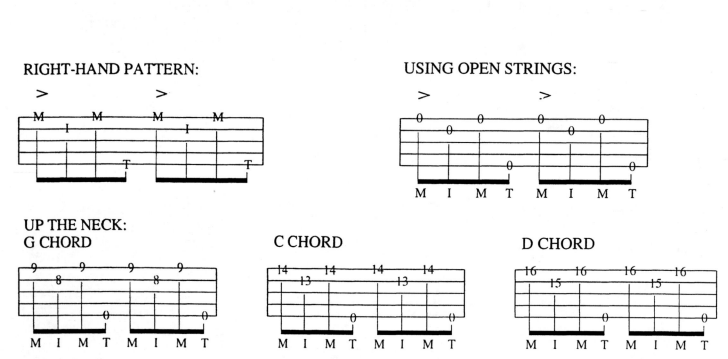

10

3. THE FORWARD-REVERSE ROLL

The *forward-reverse roll* is also a very popular roll pattern for playing up the neck of the banjo. It can be used to add "drive" to up-tempo songs and is also very effective for songs played at slower tempos. (With slower songs, every other note should receive emphasis.) Notice that the right-hand pattern rolls in one direction for four notes and then reverses the fingering order for the last four notes of the pattern. The right thumb usually plays the melody notes when playing this pattern.

RIGHT-HAND PATTERN:

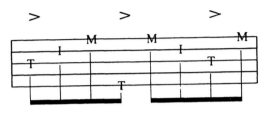

USING OPEN STRINGS:

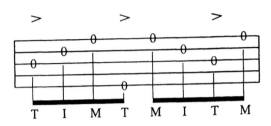

UP THE NECK:
G CHORD

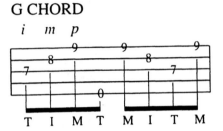

C CHORD

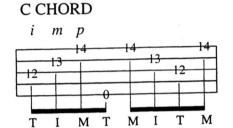

D CHORD

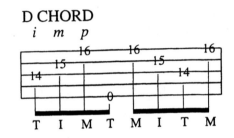

3A. ALTERNATE FORWARD-REVERSE ROLL

The *alternate forward-reverse roll* pattern is commonly used at the end of a phrase to fill in the space and to give the song the feeling of continuation. Many fill-in licks are based upon this roll pattern. (This roll is used so often, both up and down the neck, that it probably deserves its own title.)

RIGHT-HAND PATTERN:

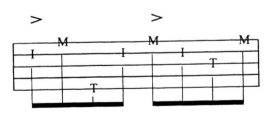

USING OPEN STRINGS:

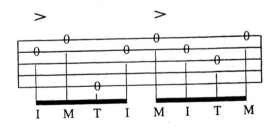

UP THE NECK:
G CHORD

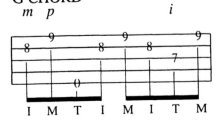

C CHORD

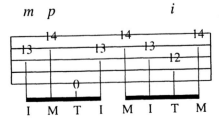

D CHORD

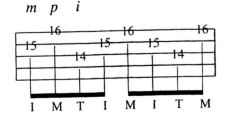

11

4. THE BACKWARD ROLL

Although the *backward roll* pattern can be played as the primary roll pattern for a song, it is more commonly used to emphasize a particular area or passage in a song when another roll pattern is used as the primary pattern. When it is combined with the forward roll pattern, the change in the fingering order in which the strings are picked is very effective for calling attention to a specific chord or for a passage where the song stays on the same chord for several bars (measures). (When played as a primary roll pattern, the middle finger plays the melody notes.)

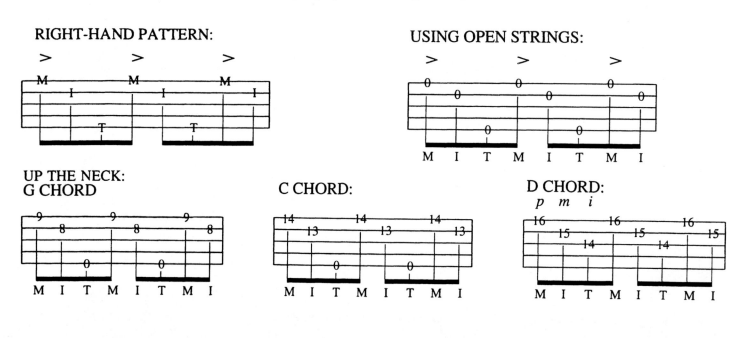

4A. ALTERNATE BACKWARD ROLL (TWO-MEASURE PATTERN)

The *alternate backward roll* pattern is a variation of the above pattern. Earl Scruggs developed this pattern to add color to specific passages in many songs (e.g., the C chord in "Bugle Call Rag," the G chord in "Lonesome Road Blues," the C chord in "Shucking the Corn," etc.) Notice that the brief forward roll at the end of measure 1 adds contrast to the fingering order, resulting in a slightly different rhythmic "feeling" from this pattern. (Usually, the left hand holds a 7th chord with this pattern.) Notice that the 2nd measure is the pure backward roll beginning with the fifth string.

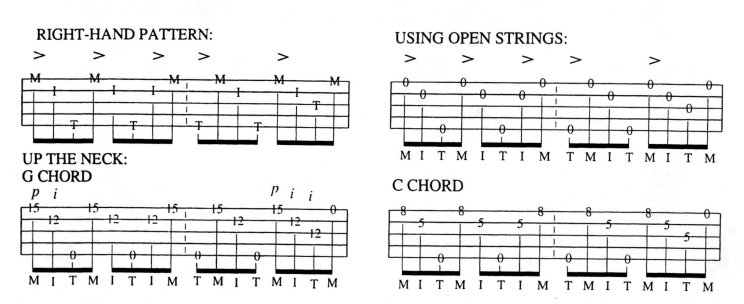

For practice: Play each roll pattern over and over several times in a row. Then try to combine several of the patterns without a break in your rhythm. Next, play each pattern with the right hand while holding a different chord position with the left hand.

The following arrangements for "Bile 'Em Cabbage" are intended to demonstrate the fact that the roll patterns and the different chord positions are tools you can use to play any song. Which ones you choose to play a song with are up to you. Each individual song can be played in many *different* ways.

Bile 'Em Cabbage Down

- *Using the alternate forward roll pattern for each measure.*
- *Notice that the left hand is working from partial chord positions.*
- *Notice that the melody notes are played on the second string.*

Traditional

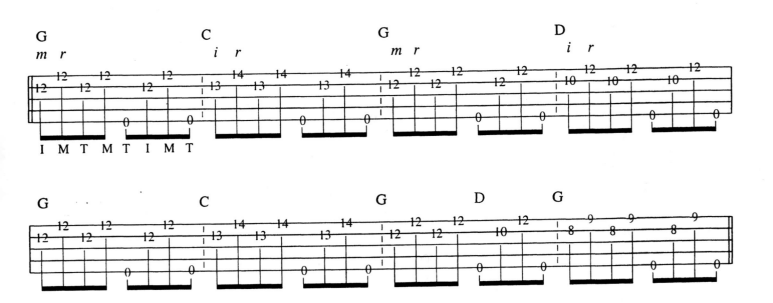

Bile 'Em Cabbage Down

- *Using the basic forward roll pattern for each measure.*

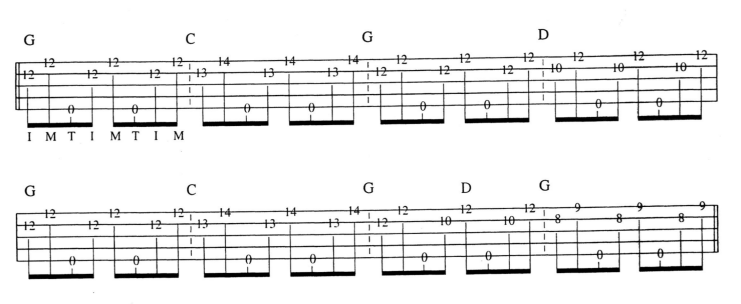

Bile 'Em Cabbage Down

• *Using the backward roll pattern for each measure.*

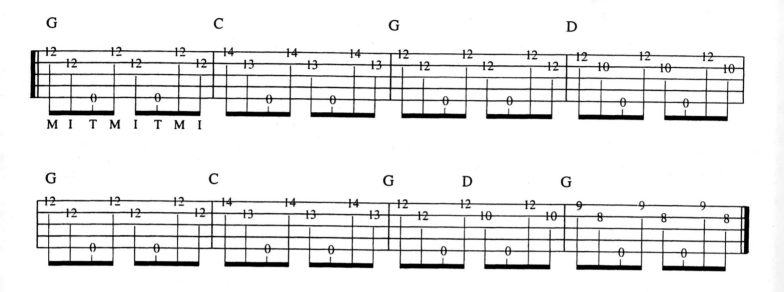

Bile 'Em Cabbage Down

• *Using the forward-reverse roll pattern and different chord positions.*

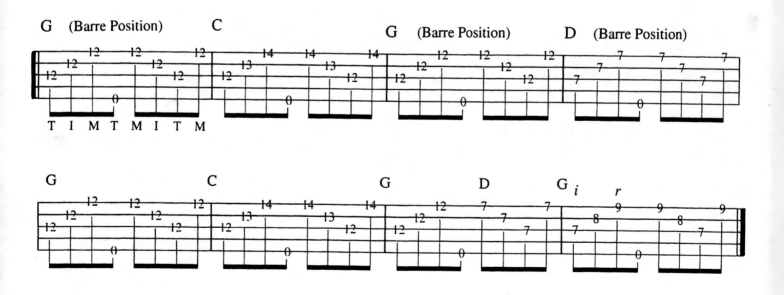

Note: You can also play a *different* roll pattern for each measure. The trick is to avoid using the same finger twice in a row when you change rolls.

The alternate forward roll pattern is a very popular roll for playing up the neck. The first arrangement below uses this roll for each measure. For fun, substitute the backward roll, or a different roll, for the A chord to create a different arrangement. The second arrangement below uses a combination of the backward and forward rolls, creating a variation of the first arrangement. Remember to keep your right hand in the Y position — away from the bridge.

Salty Dog Blues

- *Using the alternate forward roll for each measure.*

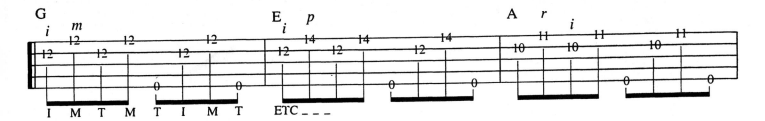

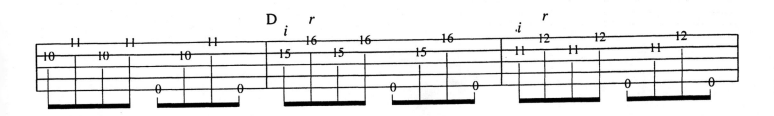

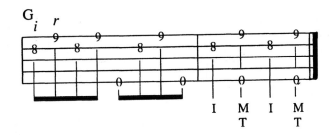

Salty Dog Blues

- *Using the backward roll and the alternate forward roll.*

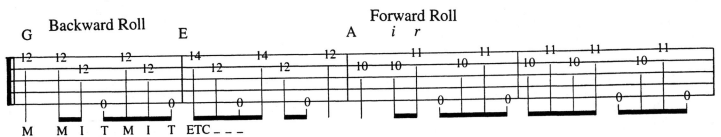

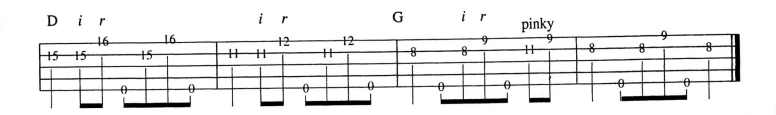

15

SUMMARY
ROLL PATTERNS

Roll patterns are right-hand fingering patterns which provide the foundation for playing the three-finger style of bluegrass banjo. Essentially every song that is played in this style can be broken down into right-hand roll patterns. As a result, these patterns are primarily responsible for providing a song with the "bluegrass sound."

NOTES:

1. Each "roll pattern" is a *right-hand fingering pattern*. The name of the roll pattern is determined by the order in which the fingers follow one another when picking the strings. (The *pattern* designates the direction your right-hand fingers "roll.") Any finger can begin the roll pattern, and the roll pattern can begin with any string.

2. Generally, one right-hand finger will play the melody notes, while the other two fingers play background notes which are determined by the chords to the song.

3. The accent mark (>) indicates which notes to emphasize. (These will generally be melody notes.)

4. Each roll consists of *eight equal counts*. All eight notes in a roll pattern should be played consecutively, *without a pause*. Also, when playing two or more roll patterns in a row, there should be no break in the rhythm. In other words, do not pause between the two patterns, and do not pause or break rhythm while playing a single pattern.

5. Each roll pattern can be played with the right hand, while holding *any* chord with the left hand.

6. Although songs generally consist of combinations of different rolls and licks, technically an entire song could be played using only one roll pattern, by playing it over and over for each chord.

It will help you in your improvisational ability to work out songs from simple melodies, to become familiar with the standard roll patterns, and to realize that much of the bluegrass sound is a result of these patterns.

CHORDS
INTRODUCTION

It is important to realize, when playing a song up the neck of the banjo, that the *left hand* is usually working from *chord positions*. Once you realize that there are only four basic positions to work from, this becomes easy.

The following chord patterns are the most common left-hand positions for songs which are played up the neck of the banjo. Almost all basic bluegrass arrangements played up the neck work from these chord positions. All of the roll patterns can be played while holding any of these chord positions. Also, all other chords (minor, diminished, augmented, etc.) can be found from each of these positions.

Each pattern is a "moveable" pattern. In other words, as each pattern is moved up or down the fingerboard, the chord will change names. The left hand moves to a different spot on the fingerboard but remains in the same formation (pattern) to play each different chord. For example, the *F position* chord pattern plays an F chord when it is in the first position on the fingerboard; move up 2 frets, and it becomes a G chord (in the F position). The name of the chord is determined by where the pattern is held by the left hand on the fingerboard. As you work through each pattern individually in the following pages, you will find that as each pattern moves up the fingerboard the chords change names in alphabetical order.

I might also mention that, in songs, you will frequently hold only a "partial" position on only two of the strings, rather than on all four. However, it is important to learn these as full chord positions.

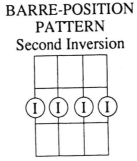

Keep in mind when working through each pattern in the following pages that:

1. Correct left-hand fingering is important. The "licks" and fancier roll patterns will work from the fingering indicated for the chord positions.

2. Any major chord can be played with each left-hand pattern.

3. The chords change names alphabetically as the left hand moves up the fingerboard.

4. The banjo repeats the same chord every 12 frets, e.g., the G chord in the F position is played at the 5th fret, and again at the 17th fret (12 frets higher).

CHORDS

It is not necessary to learn every position of every chord in order to begin playing the banjo up the neck using the higher fret numbers. However, it is important to realize that the left hand is working from chord positions and that each roll pattern or lick is being played for a specific chord.

A song is built primarily with a melody (tune) and a chord progression (series of chords). The melody (tune) for a song is built to be used with specific chords. Therefore, up-the-neck arrangements must work with chord positions. When a song is played on the deeper tones of the banjo, it frequently uses the open strings; therefore, it may not be as obvious that the song is working from chord positions. However, when a song is played up the neck of the banjo, the left hand must hold chord positions in order to work with the tones which will work for the required chords.

NOTES:

1. It is not necessary to know these chord positions to begin working with the roll patterns and licks discussed throughout this book, or to begin working with the songs. However, you should work with these chord positions frequently until you do know them. Chords are the foundation upon which all songs are built, and it will help to understand them when working out your own arrangements. Also, a knowledge of the chord positions for specific chords will aid you in playing the licks correctly with the left hand.

2. The left hand will not always hold the full chord position to play a lick (holding all four strings) but instead will often work from a partial chord position (holding the position on only two or three of the strings).

3. When playing through the examples of licks, notice that the left hand almost always works from a chord position.

4. Left-hand fingering is important with each chord position.

5. It is helpful to realize that chord positions which do not include any open strings can be moved up or down the fingerboard. As they are moved up or down the fingerboard, the name of the chord changes alphabetically.

6. A chord position which does not include open strings is usually referred to as a "closed" chord position or as a "moveable" chord position.

7. Refer to the back of this book for complete chord charts.

THE STANDARD
CHORD PATTERNS

The following chord patterns are the most commonly used left-hand positions for songs which are played up the neck of the banjo. As each pattern is moved up or down the fingerboard, the chord will change names. *Any* major chord can be played with each left-hand pattern.

When first learning the fingerboard positions for specific chords, notice in particular the location of the G chord, the C chord, and the D chord. These are the main chords used for songs which are played in the key of G. The other chords can be found alphabetically from one of these positions. For example, the A chord is located 2 frets higher than the G chord; the F chord is located 2 frets lower than the G chord, etc.

Remember: The musical alphabet ranges from A through G and then repeats so that A follows G.

Chords are the foundation upon which all songs are built. It will help to understand them when working out your own arrangements. Also, a knowledge of the chord positions will aid you in playing the rolls and licks correctly with the left hand.

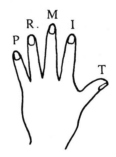

F-POSITION PATTERN
(Root Position)

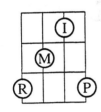

This pattern is referred to as the "F position" because the F chord is the first chord to be played in this left-hand position.

CHORDS:

F	F#	G	G#	A	A#	B	C	C#	D	D#	E	F	F#	G	G#	A	A#	B	C
3	4	5	6	7	8	9	10	11	12	13	14	15	16	17	18	19	20	21	22
2	3	4	5	6	7	8	9	10	11	12	13	14	15	16	17	18	19	20
2	3	4	5	6	7	8	9	10	11	12	13	14	15	16	17	18	19	20	21
3	4	5	6	7	8	9	10	11	12	13	14	15	16	17	18	19	20	21	22

The following "lick" is played with the left hand in the F position of the chord, while the right hand works with the forward roll pattern:

LICK: C

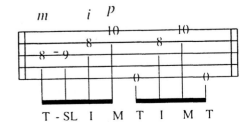

LICK: D

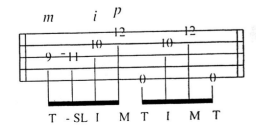

D-POSITION PATTERN
(First Inversion)

This pattern is referred to as the "D position" because the D chord is played in the first position (if you don't count D♭).

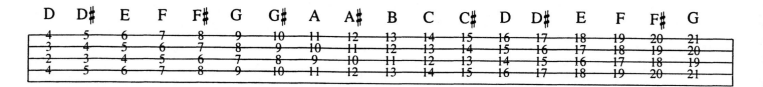

The following licks work from the D position of the chord with the left hand while the right hand works with the mixed roll pattern:

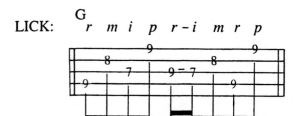

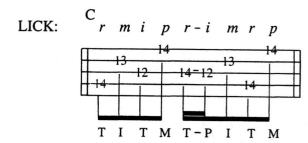

BARRE-POSITION PATTERN
(Second Inversion)

This pattern is referred to as the "barre position" because the left hand uses one finger as a bar across all four strings on the same fret.

CHORD
NAME:

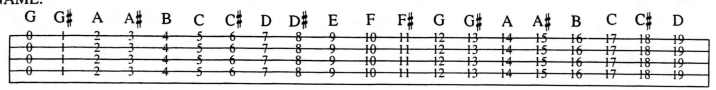

The following licks work from the barre position with the left hand while the right hand plays the backward roll pattern:

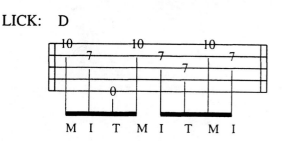

E-MINOR CHORD PATTERN

This left-hand chord pattern is frequently used for licks which are played in the up-the-neck area of the banjo. The E-minor chord is held by the left hand in this position for many licks which are played for the G chord. (The E-minor chord is the relative minor of the G chord.)

Because E minor is the chord most commonly played with this left-hand position, the position is referred to as the "E-minor pattern." However, the first chord that can be played in this position is the A-minor chord. The Am chord is often held for C-chord licks. Likewise, the Dm chord is often held for F-chord licks. (These chords are indicated in parentheses beneath the minor-chord name.)

CHORDS:

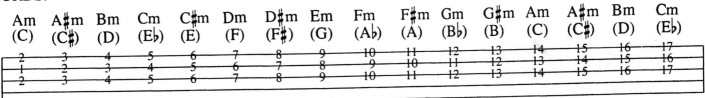

The following licks work from the E-minor position of the chord with the left hand, while the right hand works with the forward-reverse* roll pattern. (When playing the licks, the left pinky finger usually reaches for chromatic tones, which are located outside of the chord position.)

LICK:
G

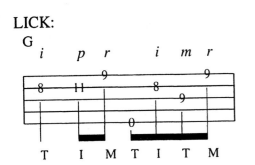

LICK:
C

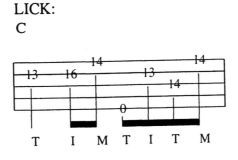

LICK:
F

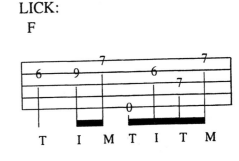

*Alternate forward-reverse roll variation.

*NOTES_____
1. The E-minor position can be used for minor chords and for major chords.
2. ♯ means to "sharp" or raise (in pitch) 1 fret. Therefore, any chord with this symbol following the letter will be located 1 fret above the position of the chord letter, i.e., G♯ is located 1 fret position above the G chord.
3. ♭ means to "flat" or lower (in pitch) 1 fret. Therefore, any chord with this symbol following the letter will be located 1 fret lower than the regular position for this chord, i.e., B♭ is located 1 fret lower (in pitch) than B.

When the tune "Cumberland Gap" is played on the banjo, the B section is normally played up the neck. When playing through the following arrangement, hold the E-minor chord position with your left hand throughout the entire up-the-neck section (Part B). The left pinky is used to reach the 11th fret, while the other fingers continue to hold the Em position. Notice that the right hand is playing roll patterns.

Cumberland Gap

- *Standard variation.*

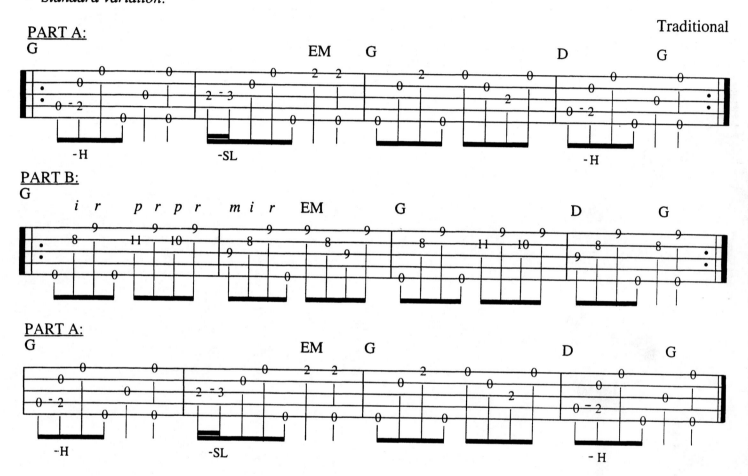

ALTERNATE PART B
- *Using the basic forward roll for the 1st and 3rd measures.*

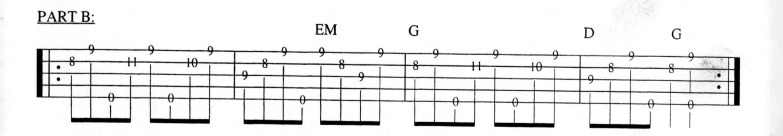

It is essential to understand that even though you are playing on only two strings of the banjo, you are nevertheless playing a chord. It is simply referred to as a "partial" chord position when the left hand holds only two or three strings. "Train 45" begins with 4 measures of a G chord. This is a very common beginning for many bluegrass songs, and the techniques which are used to play this song can also be applied to those songs.

Train 45

- *This is a standard arrangement using the lower-pitched tones of the banjo to establish the tune.*
- *This song is identified by the licks and the chord progression. Notice the similarity of the beginning with that of "Foggy Mountain Breakdown."*

Traditional

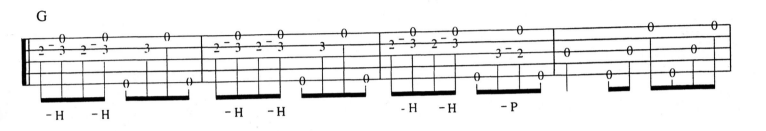

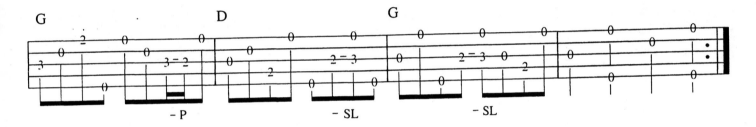

Train 45

- *Up-the-neck arrangement using a different position for the G chord in each measure.*
- *Notice that the left hand holds only two strings (partial position).*
- *The first 4 measures can be substituted for the first 4 measures of "Foggy Mountain Breakdown" or any other tune beginning with 4 measures of G.*

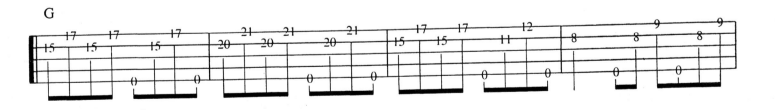

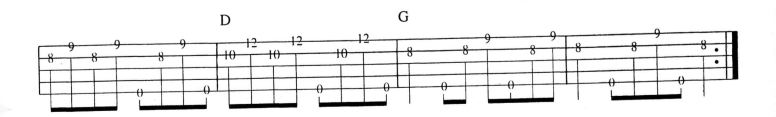

23

It is helpful to realize that the banjo fingerboard repeats itself, beginning with the 12th fret. In other words, the 12th fret acts as the nut of the banjo, and the same chord positions located down the neck can be found up the neck using this relationship. Compare the up-the-neck arrangements on the following page to the standard arrangements for "John Hardy" (below). Notice the relationship of the left-hand positions for the C chord in each arrangement.

John Hardy

- *Standard arrangement played down the neck in order to establish the melody.*
- *Compare the left-hand and right-hand patterns with the up-the-neck arrangements.*

Traditional

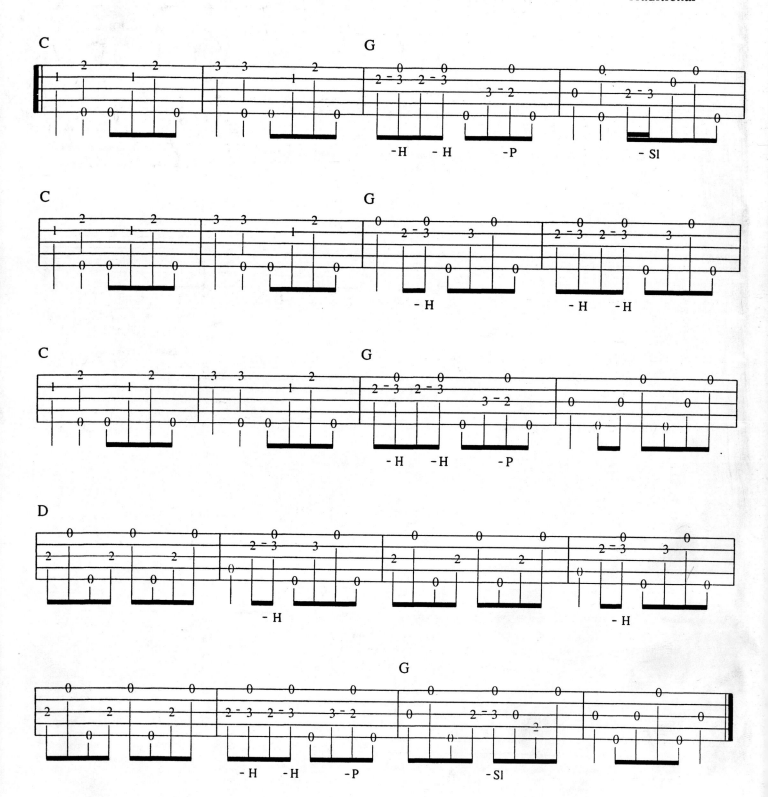

John Hardy

- *Up the neck using the alternate forward roll for each measure with the right hand .*
- *Holding partial chord positions with the left hand (two strings instead of four).*

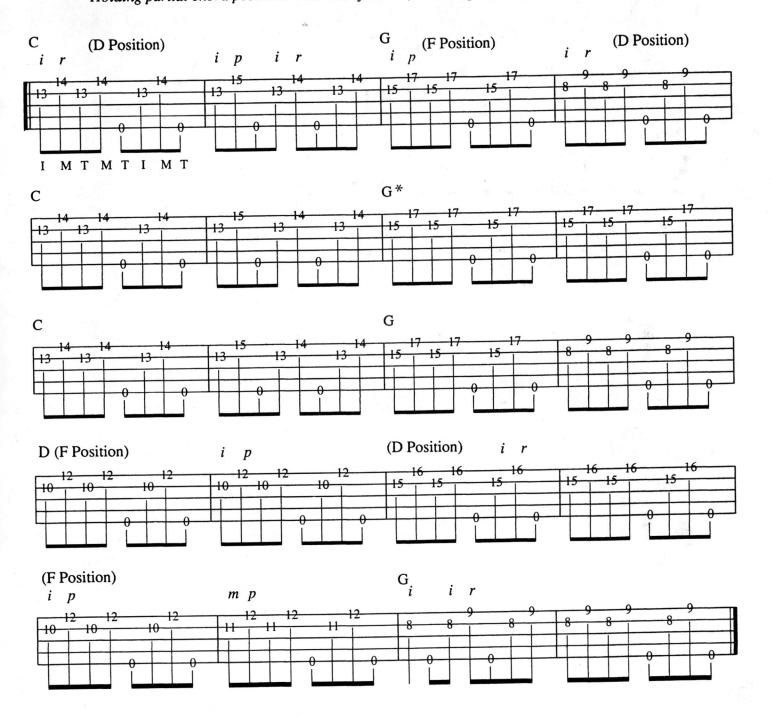

ALTERNATE POSITION

- *Substitute for the G chord (measures 7 and 8) in the above arrangement. Remember, when you are working out an arrangement up the neck, you can choose the chord position that sounds best to your ear and use the roll pattern you prefer to play.*

G*

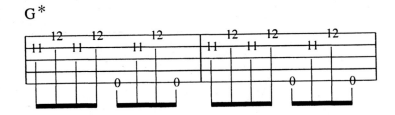

John Hardy

- *Advanced variation using roll patterns and emphasizing the potential of chords.*
- *Notice the substitute chords used for the D chord. These add more color to the arrangement and help to drive the music back to the G chord.*
- *Notice that different roll patterns are used for the D chord than were used in the previous variation. You can use any roll you choose when working out your own arrangements.*

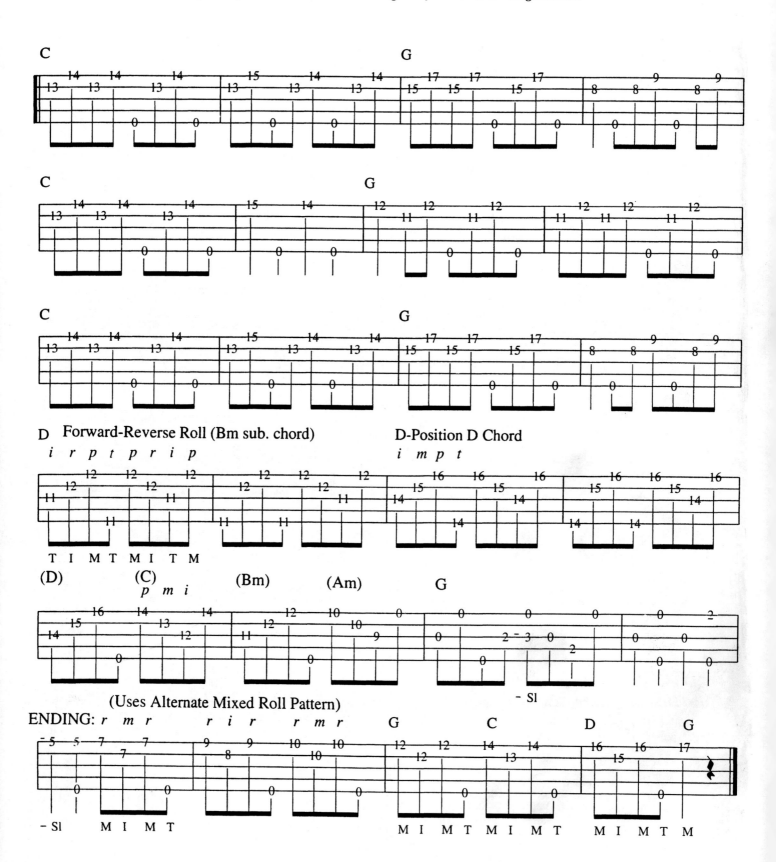

The F chord is played 2 frets lower than the G chord in each of the chord position patterns. This chord is found in many bluegrass songs and creates a modal effect when used with the G chord. Therefore, playing up the neck often involves the use of the F chord. For practice: Find all of the F-chord locations on the fingerboard.

Little Maggie

- *Standard arrangement played down the neck in order to establish the melody. Compare the right- and left-hand patterns with the up-the-neck arrangements chord by chord and measure by measure.*

Traditional

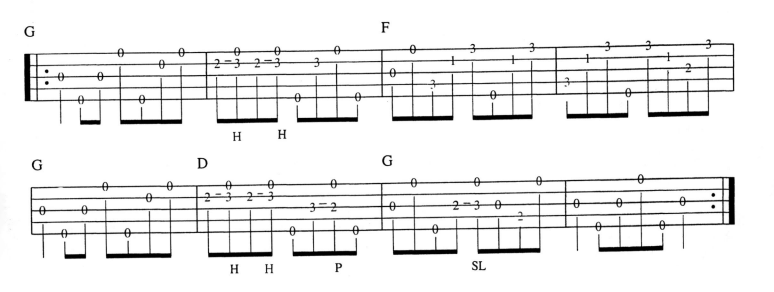

Little Maggie

- *Up-the-neck arrangement.*
- *The first 2 measures use different positions for the G chord; the left hand is holding partial chords (two strings).*

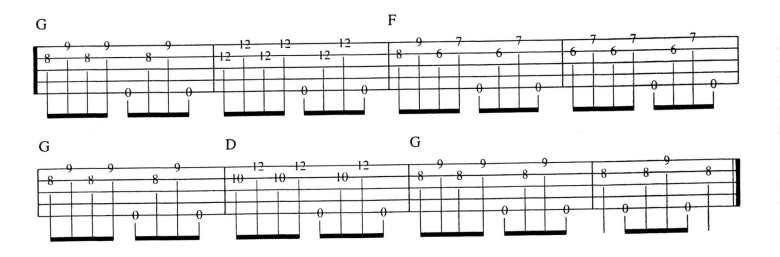

Little Maggie

- *Up-the-neck arrangement using different positions for the G and D chords.*

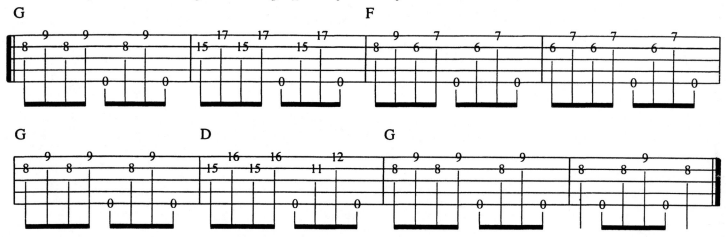

Little Maggie

- *Up-the-neck arrangement using the barre position for the F chord.*

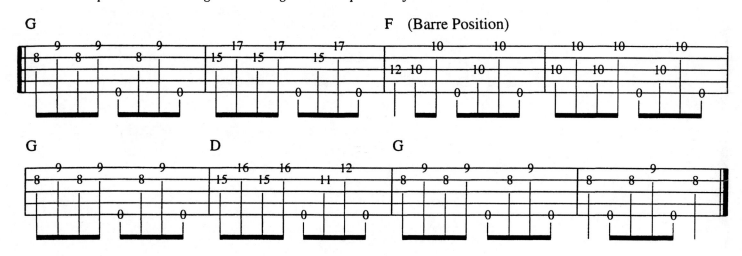

Little Maggie

- *Up-the-neck arrangement substituting the <u>F position</u> for the G and F chords.*
- *Notice that some of the tune is absent; this is fine for a second variation and often adds energy to the song.*

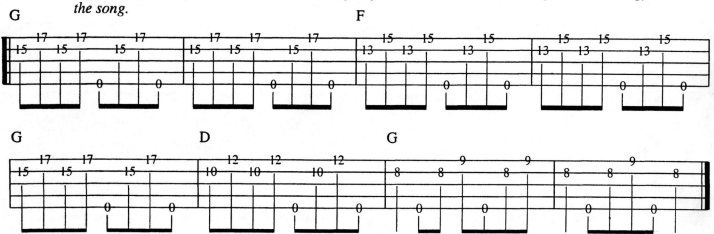

Remember, this should be your arrangement. If you feel something different, do it. Try using your **pinky** for the first and third notes, 4th measure in the top arrangement, on the 9th fret.

28

Each of the following arrangements uses a single chord pattern throughout to emphasize the fact that the placement of the pattern on the fingerboard determines the name (and sound) of each specific chord. This also demonstrates that the same pattern can be used for every chord in a song. Again, remember that up-the-neck arrangements do not have to carry a strong sense of melody. Notice also that each arrangement uses the same roll pattern throughout.

Note: The chord progression (order) follows the circle of 5ths. "Salty Dog," "Dear Old Dixie," and many other songs use a similar progression. (Pay special attention to the locations for the D chord, for this chord is played in almost every song played on the banjo.)

Don't Let the Deal Go Down

- *Using the barre position for each chord.*
- *Using the forward-reverse roll for each measure.*
- *Note: When you reach the repeat sign, return to the pick-up notes and repeat the entire variation. The chord progression should be played twice.*

Traditional — Key of G

Pick-up notes:

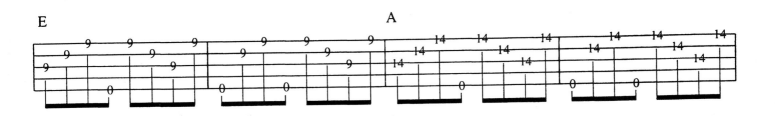

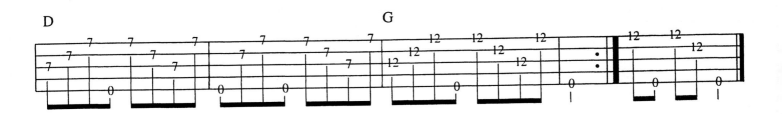

Note: You can also combine two different variations to form one arrangement, rather than repeating the same arrangement.

Don't Let the Deal Go Down
Up the Neck #2

- *Using the **D position** for each chord.*
- *The left **thumb** is often used to fret the fifth string when songs are played up the neck of the banjo.*

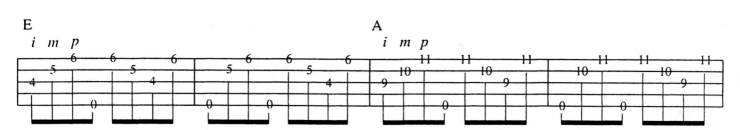

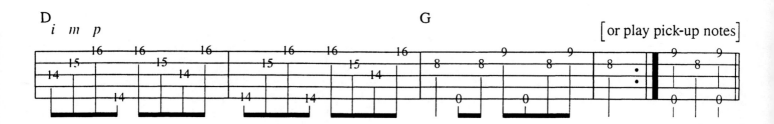

Don't Let the Deal Go Down
Up the Neck #3

- *Using the **F position** for each chord until the final G chord.*
- *For practice, substitute the G chord in the F position (last 2 measures).*

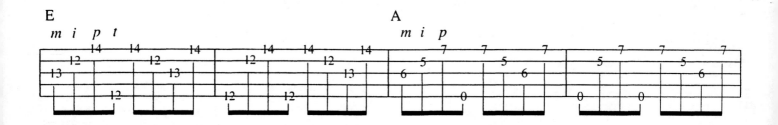

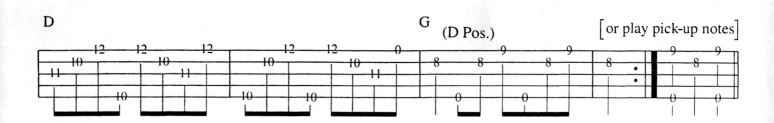

The C chord is used in many different songs. The following arrangement is intended to familiarize you with the up-the-neck positions for this chord.

Wildwood Flower

- *Hold the chords throughout this arrangement with the left hand.*
- *Use the left **ring** finger to alternate between the strings.*

Traditional — Key of C

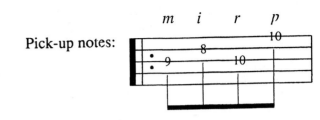

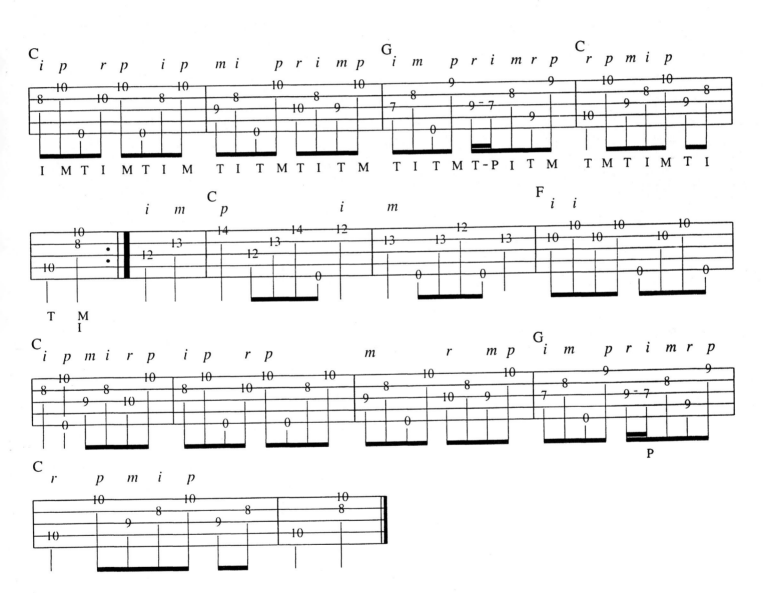

Note: Move each left-hand position up 2 frets (in number), and play the same strings with the right hand. You will now be playing in the key of D, beginning with the D chord. Move each left-hand position up 2 frets again, and play the same patterns with the right hand to play the song in the key of E. Begin with the G chord (F position) and follow the same relationship to play in the key of G. This is the procedure referred to as "transposing."

This well-known tune is played in the key of A minor (with the banjo in standard G tuning). Notice that a different chord is played for each measure but that the same right-hand pattern can be used for each chord. (Quarter notes are used for rhythmic variety.)

The House of the Rising Sun

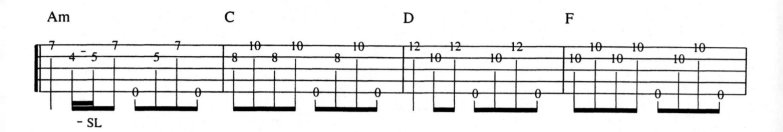

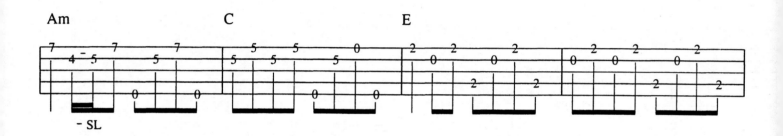

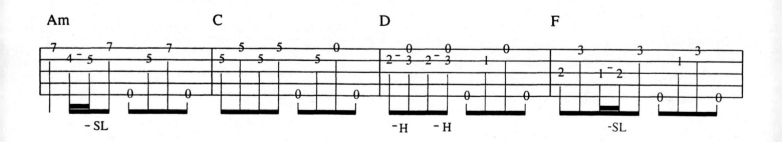

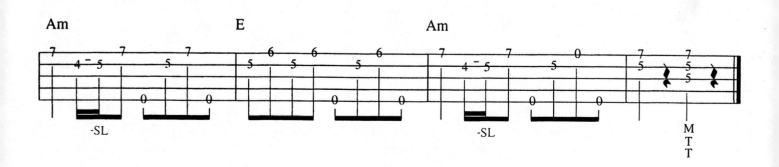

SUMMARY
CHORDS

It is helpful to know the chord positions, particularly for specific chords which are used frequently in songs played on the banjo, for several reasons:

1. Almost everything that is played up the neck of the banjo works from chord positions with the left hand. This may often involve holding only partial chords (e.g., holding only two or three strings) as well as "full" chord positions (fretting all four strings).

2. Roll patterns are played with the right hand, while chord positions are held with the left hand, when songs are played up the neck. (The melody notes almost always can be found either within the chord position or nearby.)

3. Each lick (covered in the next section) is to be played for a specific chord. Holding the chord position with the left hand will facilitate playing the lick correctly. It is almost always easier to play a lick if the left hand is holding the chord position required for the lick.

4. Most of the chords which are played on the banjo can be played from one of four left-hand patterns. The following chart shows the fingerboard locations for the most commonly played chords. (See the back of this book for complete chord charts.)

FINGERBOARD LOCATIONS FOR COMMONLY PLAYED CHORDS

F POSITION:

[G]
```
5        17
3        15
4        16
5        17
```

[C]
```
10
8
9
10
```

[D]
```
12
10
11
12
```

D POSITION:

[G]
```
9
8
7
9
```

[C]
```
2        14
1        13
0        12
2        14
```

[D]
```
4        16
3        15
2        14
4        16
```

BARRE POSITION:

[G]
```
0        12
0        12
0        12
0        12
```

[C]
```
5        17
5        17
5        17
5        17
```

[D]
```
7        19
7        19
7        19
7        19
```

Em POSITION:

[Em]
```
9
8
9
```

[Am]
```
2        14
1        13
2        14
```

[Bm]
```
4        16
3        15
4        16
```

33

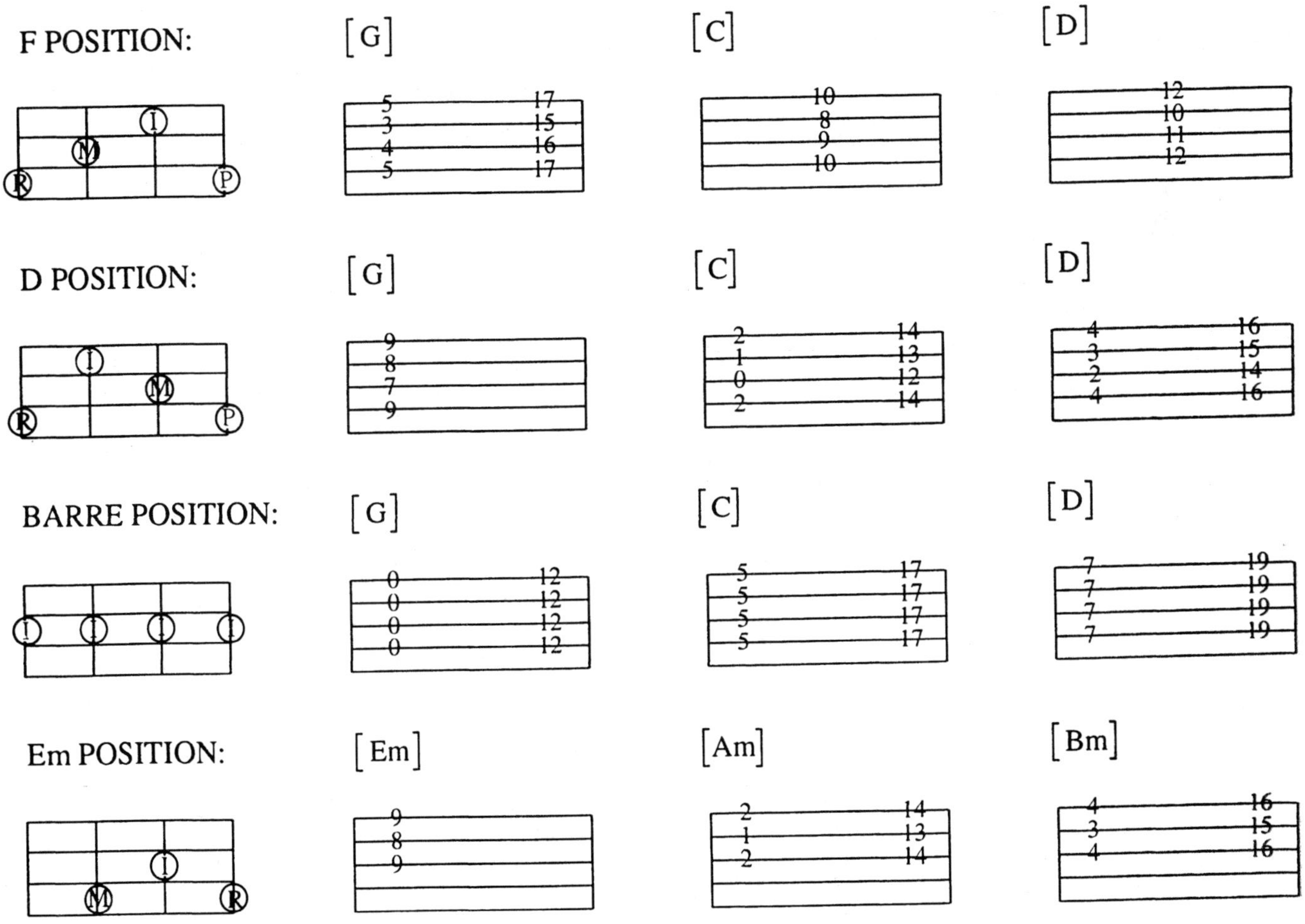

LICKS
INTRODUCTION

Licks are the patterns that add *polish* to the sound of a bluegrass-style arrangement. Although licks are based upon the right-hand roll patterns, they also involve the use of the left hand. Licks frequently make use of the various left-hand techniques, such as the hammer, sliding from one note to another, bending the strings with the left hand, etc. They also utilize techniques such as chromaticism by inserting non-chord tones into the pattern. *Unlike the roll patterns, which can be played while holding any chord position with the left hand, each lick is to be played only for a certain chord.*

Most up-the-neck arrangements involve playing a combination of licks which are chosen according to the chords for the song. When playing through the examples of licks in the following pages, it will help to keep the following in mind:

1. Most up-the-neck arrangements involve playing a combination of licks which are chosen according to the *chords* for the song.

2. Each lick is played *only* for a specific chord.

3. The *left hand* generally works from chord positions when playing licks on the higher tones of the banjo.

4. The right hand frequently picks specific patterns when playing up-the-neck licks. (Try to identify the roll pattern used for each lick. Also, notice the variations of the rolls.)

5. An accent, or strong emphasis, should often be placed on the first note of each lick. (This is frequently a melody note and is in keeping with the natural rhythm of music.)

6. Each lick consists of eight equal counts (one measure of music or tablature). If there are only seven notes in one lick, it will be necessary to "pause" after one of the notes to allow for the eight beats in the measure (one measure = eight eighth notes).

7. Each lick may sound incomplete when it is played by itself. Each lick is resolved by the first note of the lick which follows. (Each lick will sound more complete if you follow it with the first note of another lick.)

8. Any lick can be interchanged or substituted for any other lick, as long as the licks are played for the same chord.

9. Many licks are actually moveable patterns which can be played for any chord (depending upon the left-hand position on the fingerboard).

BASIC UP-THE-NECK LICKS

The following examples are among the most commonly played licks in up-the-neck arrangements. Each of these licks can a) be used as punctuation to fill in the spaces, or b) be combined with one another according to the chords for a song, to play an entire arrangement.

I recommend that my students learn to use these licks first; then they can substitute other licks for the same chord in their arrangements. I also recommend practicing each lick as an exercise, playing it over and over, in time, emphasizing the appropriate notes.

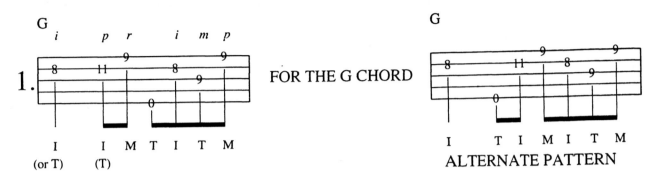

FOR THE G CHORD

Hold the E-minor chord position with the left hand and use the pinky to reach the 11th fret ("Cumberland Gap" position). This G lick is the up-the-neck version for the familiar:

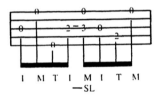

It can be used for the G chord in any up-the-neck arrangement for any song. If the song calls for 2 measures of the G chord, play this lick twice.

FOR THE C CHORD

Hold the F position of the C chord with the left hand, using the correct fingers (pinky on the first string, not the ring finger). You do not have to fret the fourth string to play this lick. A roll-pattern variation for this lick is played:

To play the lick, move the position back 1 fret, pick the third string, then slide into the C chord. (The first two notes of the lick are played in the same amount of time the first note is played in the roll pattern example.)

This lick is played both of the ways presented above. The choice is yours. Some prefer the first pattern (fast slide), while others prefer the second (slower slide).

3. FOR THE D CHORD

T-Sl M I M T I M T

D — ALTERNATE PATTERN

T-Sl I M T I M T

Notice that the C lick and D lick are alike but are played in a different place. Hold the F position for the D chord 2 frets lower (where the C chord is played), and quickly slide to the D-chord position, after picking the third string.

The above D lick is the up-the-neck equivalent of:

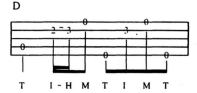

T I-H M T I M T

G, C, D

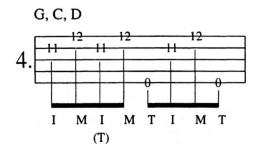

4. FOR THE G, C, & D CHORDS

(for each of these chords)

I M I M T I M T
(T)

Use the left middle and pinky fingers to play this lick. This lick works for more than one chord, even though it is played on the same fret numbers:

Played for the G chord, it flats the 3rd, which is a common technique.

Played for the C chord, it creates the C9 chord, often used for color.

Played for the D chord, it creates the D aug. chord, often used before G.

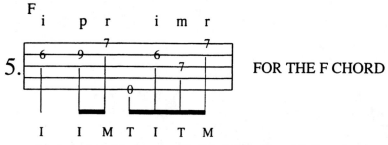

5. FOR THE F CHORD

I I M T I T M

Notice that this is actually Lick #1 played 2 frets lower.

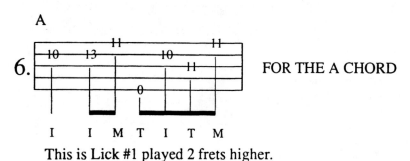

6. FOR THE A CHORD

I I M T I T M

This is Lick #1 played 2 frets higher.

Train 45

- *Using licks for the G and D chords for the final phrase.*
- *Licks are effective for adding energy to the overall effect.*

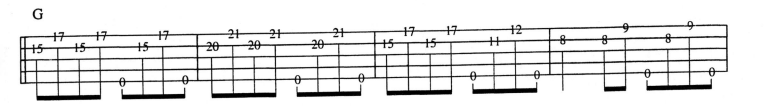

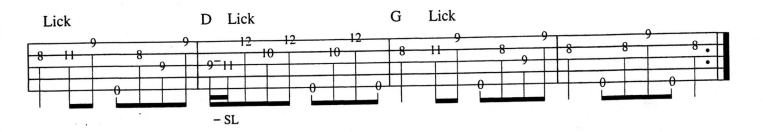

Little Maggie

- *Using licks for the F and G chords. Notice that these are the same pattern.*
- *Licks are often used to fill in the pause at the end of each phrase.*

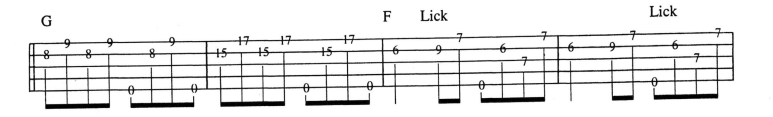

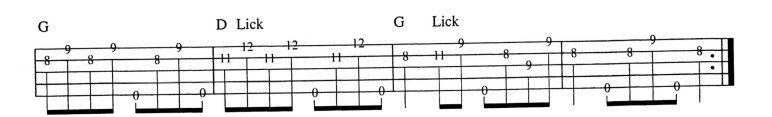

The following arrangement uses standard up-the-neck licks to play "John Hardy." Notice the C chord; look at what is played for the G chord; look at the D chord in 2-measure groups to see the patterns. These licks can be used for these chords in any song that calls for these chords. If a song calls for the C chord for 2 measures, you can play the C licks used below in that song, also. (You should use these licks until you are absolutely certain of them.)

John Hardy

• *Using standard up-the-neck licks.*

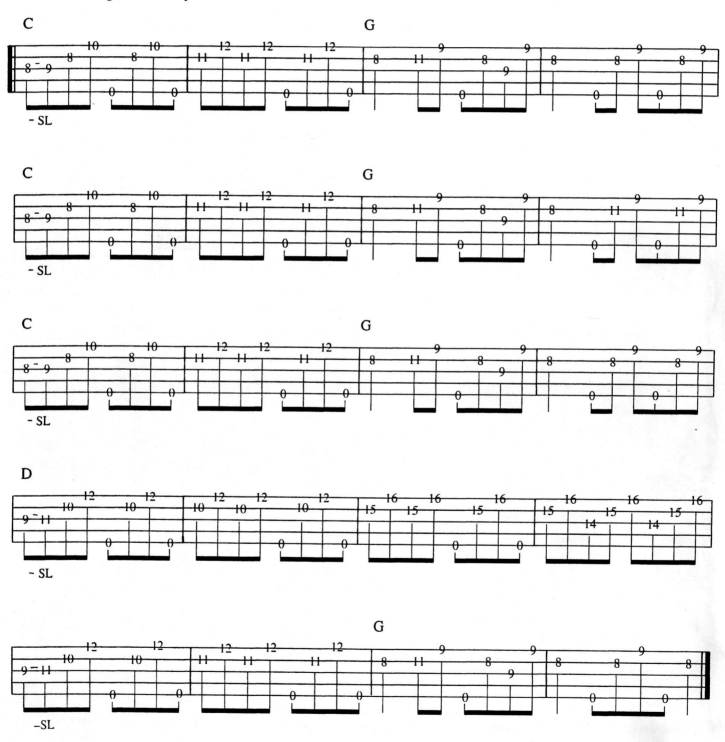

This arrangement of "Mama Don't Allow" uses a standard up-the-neck lick for almost every measure. In addition, it demonstrates an effective way to combine up-the-neck licks with down-the-neck licks, by playing the last note of the up-the-neck lick as an open string. (See measures 2–3 below.) Notice that the last note of measure 2 is played with an open string, tonally connecting the two areas of the fingerboard.

Mama Don't Allow

- *Using a standard up-the-neck lick for each measure, according to the correct chord.*
- *Travelling down the neck through an open string.*

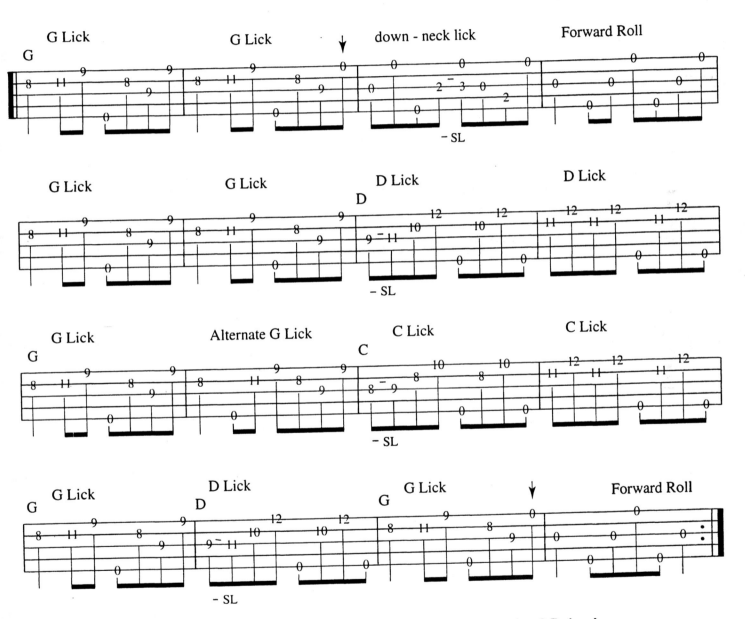

For practice: Substitute the alternate G lick for each measure of G chord.

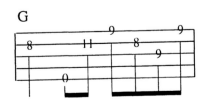

This is a gospel standard that has been recorded by many bluegrass bands. Notice that the basic right-hand pattern is the alternate forward roll pattern. The G-chord lick is used as a fill-in lick for each phrase. Also compare the C-chord and D-chord licks. (Notice that the pattern is the same, but the D chord uses the alternate form.)

Crying Holy Unto the Lord

Pick-up notes:

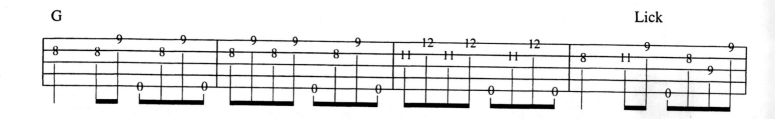

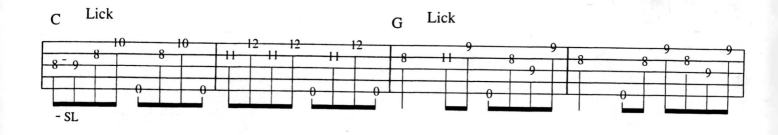

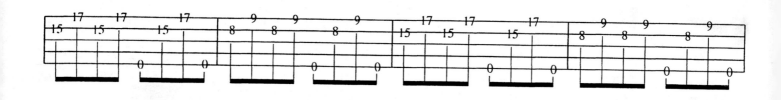

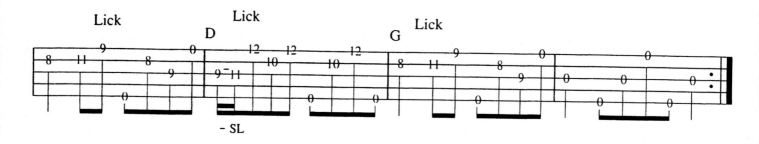

THE "IDENTITY FACTOR"

The introductory section of this book mentioned the fact that many songs which are played in the up-the-neck area of the banjo are variations, or second breaks, and that the melody or tune for the songs is not always prevalent. This book has also discussed the fact that up-the-neck arrangements are usually a combination of rolls and licks, and that the *same* patterns can be used for many *different songs*.

In addition, many bluegrass songs do not have a definitive melody. Have you ever tried to sing "Foggy Mountain Breakdown"? Did you know that "Bugle Call Rag" and "Dueling Banjos" use exactly the same chord progression and can be played using identical licks? How does the listener know which song is being played in these instances? What distinguishes one song from the other?

Instead of a noticeable melody, each of the songs of this type usually has an *identifying motif*. For example, although "Bugle Call Rag" and the fast section of "Dueling Banjos" use the same chord progression, "Bugle Call Rag" is preceded by harmonics (chimes) with an identifiable introductory section. "Dueling Banjos" is also preceded by an identifiable introduction which uses the motif for "Yankee Doodle" and which builds in tempo.

IDENTITY-FACTOR EXAMPLES

1. **BUGLE CALL RAG intro :**
   (HARMONICS)

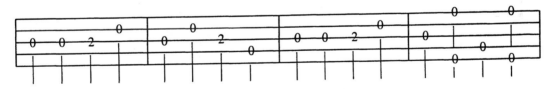

2. **DUELING BANJOS pick-up to fast part :**

3. **SHUCKING THE CORN :**

Emphasis of a particular chord can also be an identity factor for a song. For example, the long D chord in "John Hardy" distinguishes this song from others which might have the same basic chord progression. In other words, although "John Hardy" does have a strong melody, an up-the-neck arrangement can be completely void of the tune, for the long D chord will tell you it is "John Hardy."

When you are working out an arrangement for a song which doesn't seem to have a strong tune, notice both the chord progression and any particular feature the song might have as its identity factor. Play licks and roll patterns for the chords, include the factor, and you should have a valid arrangement for the song.

Again, the same licks can be used to play many different songs when playing up the neck of the banjo. If the chord progression is the same for two different songs, the same arrangement can be used to play both of them.

The following chord progression is used to play "Bugle Call Rag," "Dueling Banjos" (fast part), the beginning of the final section of "Black Mountain Rag," and many other songs. The "identity factor," if included, would be the distinguishing factor between these songs.

Chord Progression #1

- *Using the same roll pattern for each measure.*

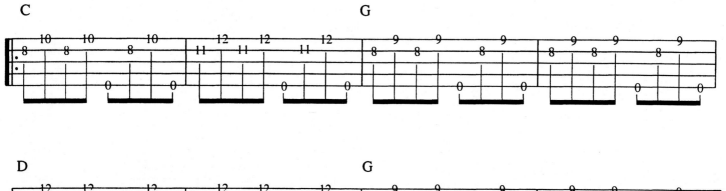

Chord Progression #2

- *Using standard up-the-neck licks for each chord.*

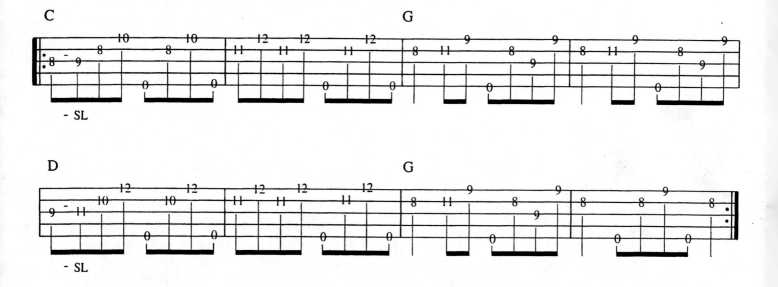

For practice: Play the "Bugle" identity factor followed by the above progression played twice. The result should be a break for "Bugle Call Rag."

The following arrangement can be played for the tune "Lonesome Road Blues" or for any other song which uses the same chord progression for the same number of measures.

1. If you change the C chord to an E-minor chord, you will have an arrangement for "Foggy Mountain Breakdown."

2. If you play an F chord instead of the C chord, you will have an arrangement for "Bluegrass Breakdown."

3. If you delete the third line, you will be playing "Shucking the Corn."

4. If you omit the second and third lines and change the first D lick (1st measure, last line) to a G lick, you will have an arrangement for "Train 45."

Chord Progression #3

- *Using standard roll patterns and licks.*

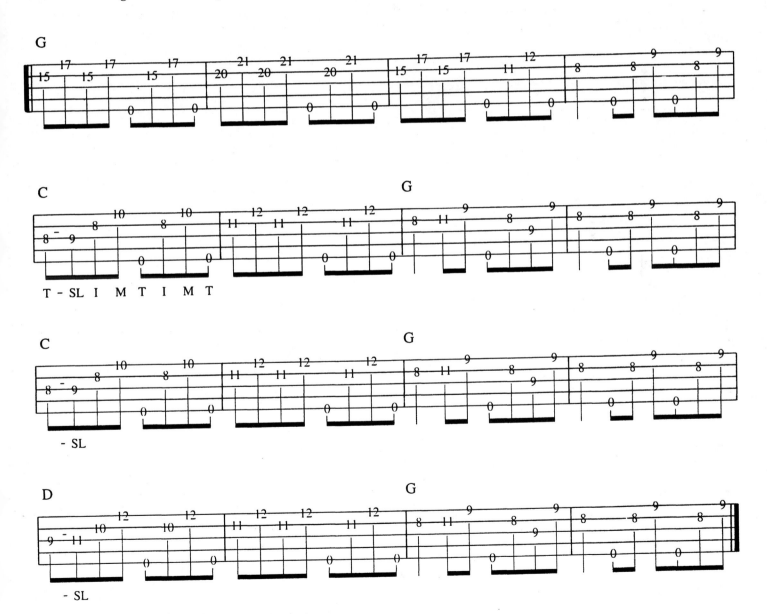

Note: Remember to keep your right hand in the Y position!

An up-the-neck arrangement will often include a hint or suggestion of the melody for a song when it has an identifiable tune, although the arrangement will consist primarily of licks. The opening bars of "Lonesome Road Blues" include the melody. From the C chord forward, the arrangement consists of licks.

Lonesome Road Blues

Traditional

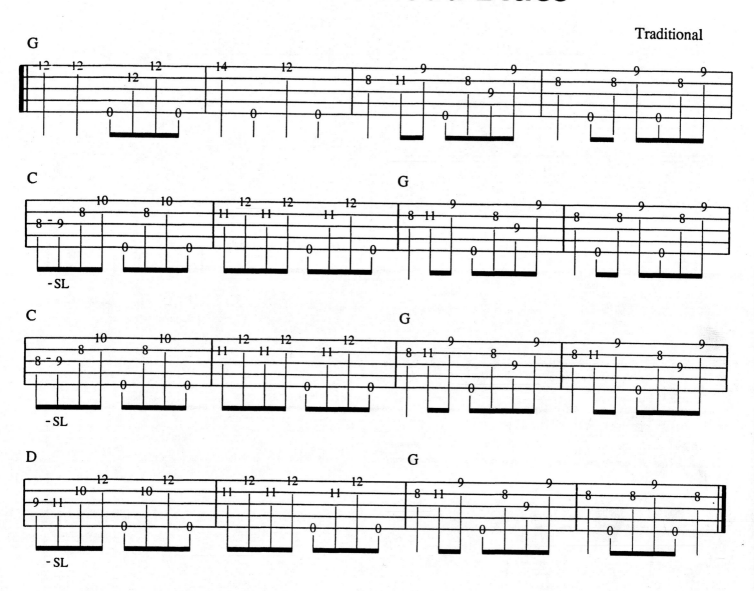

Note: You can also substitute either of the following for the 1st measure of the C chord in each line.

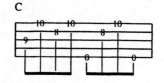

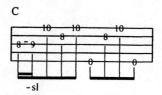

44

The following arrangement, consisting of standard roll patterns and licks, can also be used for "Mama Don't Allow" and for "New River Train," for they use the same chord progression.

The 6th measure includes a roll pattern referred to as the alternate forward-reverse in the four basic rolls. This roll pattern is very common in up-the-neck arrangements. (This pattern is often used in order to end the measure on the first string, so the right thumb can begin the next lick.)

Roll in My Sweet Baby's Arms

• *Using standard rolls and licks.*

Traditional

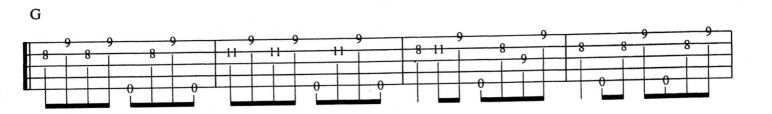

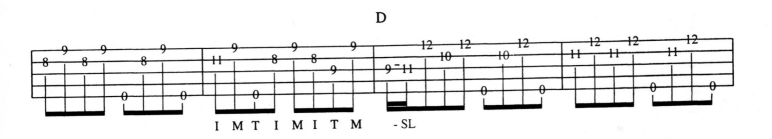

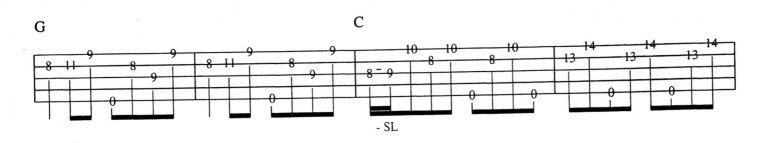

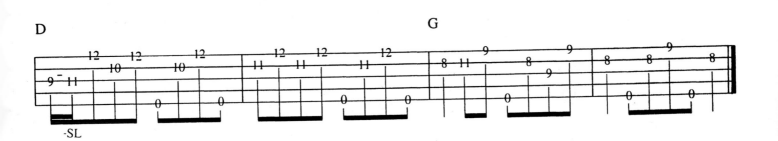

Although the arrangement on the previous page is a valid arrangement, you can also incorporate the melody for the song into the roll patterns in order to distinguish this song from others which utilize the same chord progression. (The melody is the tune you would sing; the other notes are harmony or background notes.)

Roll in My Sweet Baby's Arms

- *Incorporating the melody.*
- *Notice that the final D chord uses the same right-hand pattern used to play the D lick in the previous arrangement, but it chooses melody notes from within the chord position, rather than the slide on the third string.*

G   (or substitute lick here)

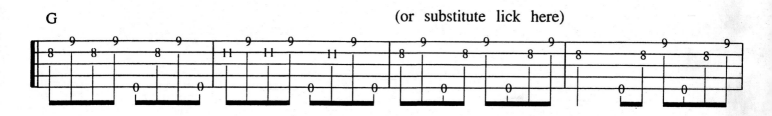

(moves to different position of G Chord)   D (or substitute lick)

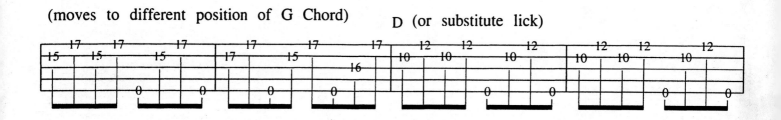

G   C

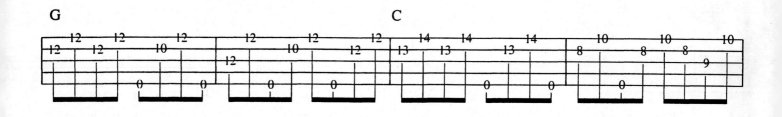

D   G (or play lick here)

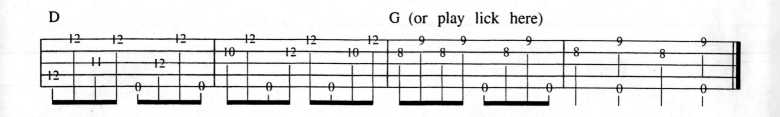

Note: There are no licks written into the above arrangement. Try substituting the licks when they are suggested above the appropriate measures.

46

ADDITIONAL LICKS
INTERCHANGEABLE LICKS BY CHORD

The licks contained in the following pages can be interchanged with the licks discussed previously, as long as they are applied to the same chord.

Technically speaking, any combination of the up-the-neck licks can be used to play a song "up the neck" of the banjo, as long as the licks are played for the correct chords at the proper time. Remember, licks can be used to play a song in its entirety, or they can be used in combination with roll patterns. Because up-the-neck arrangements are often played as second variations, there is a great deal of freedom for improvisation and variety.

Note: When deciding which lick(s) to use in an arrangement, it may help to remember that generally the first note of each lick should receive the strongest emphasis. This is frequently a melody note, or can be used to imply the melody.

PICK-UP NOTES
BEGINNING LICKS

The following licks are frequently used to begin an up-the-neck arrangement.

G LICKS

Each of the following licks can be used in any song for the G chord. Each lick is the equivalent of one measure of tablature (contains eight equal counts). Each of these licks can be interchanged with one another in a song, or it can be substituted for a roll pattern.

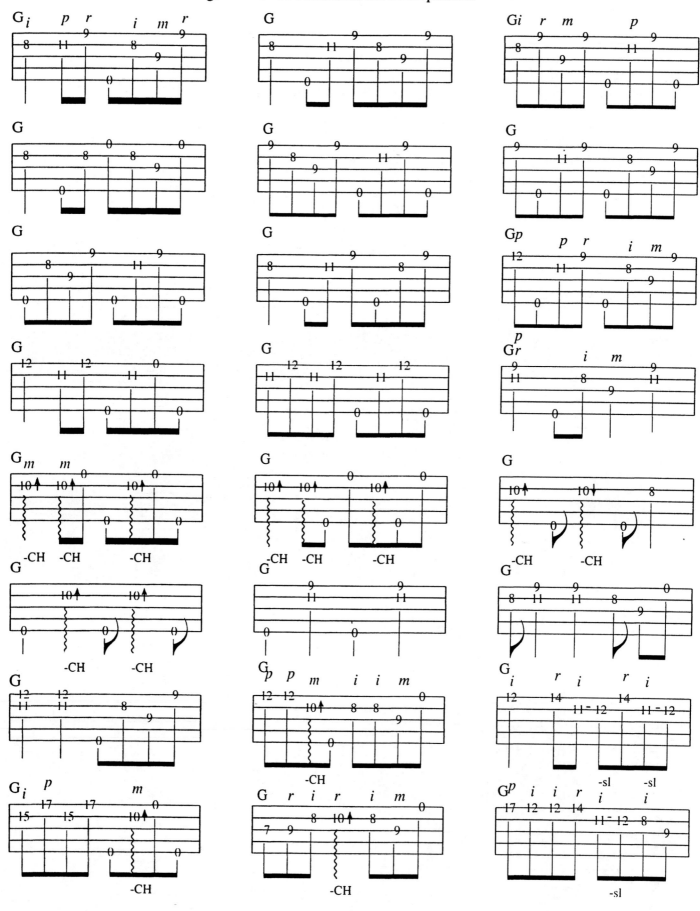

C LICKS

The C chord occurs in many songs which are played on the banjo. Each of the following licks can be played for 1 measure of the C chord any time it occurs in a song. Many of the C licks are moveable patterns — play the lick 2 frets higher and it becomes a D lick.

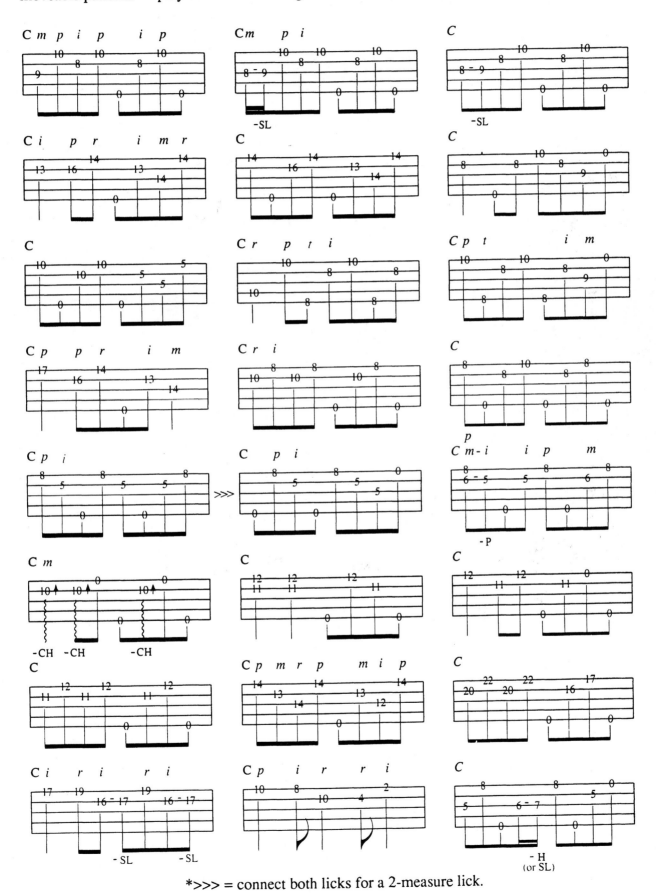

*>>> = connect both licks for a 2-measure lick.

D LICKS

Each of the following licks can be played for the D chord when it occurs in a song. The D chord is one of the most important chords used in the key of G (V chord). Generally, the D-chord licks lead the music to G-chord licks. For 2-measure licks, combine a lick from the top line with any lick from lines 2–8.

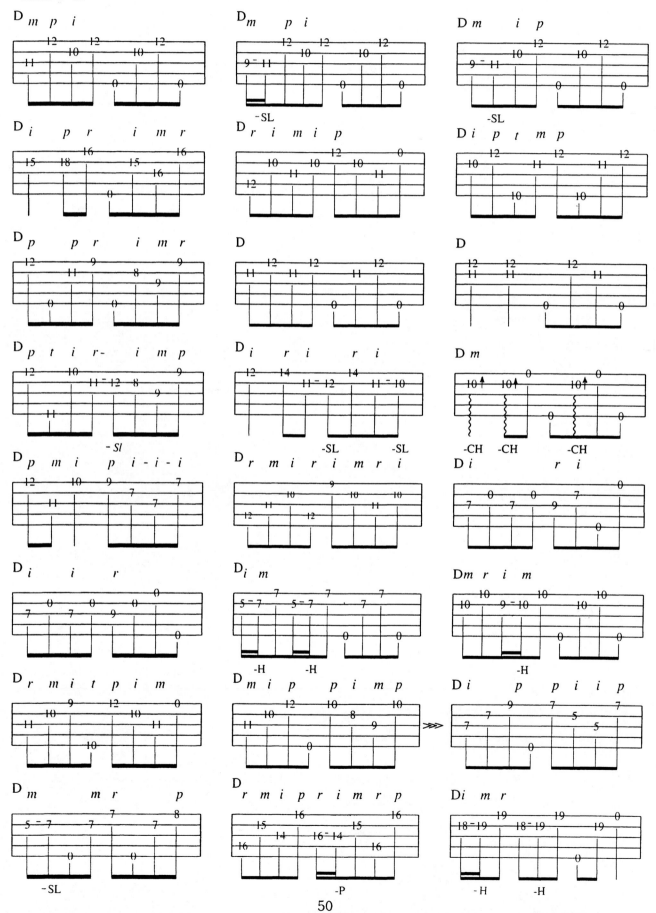

50

A LICKS

A licks are usually followed by D licks. A-chord licks are also frequently "moveable" patterns.

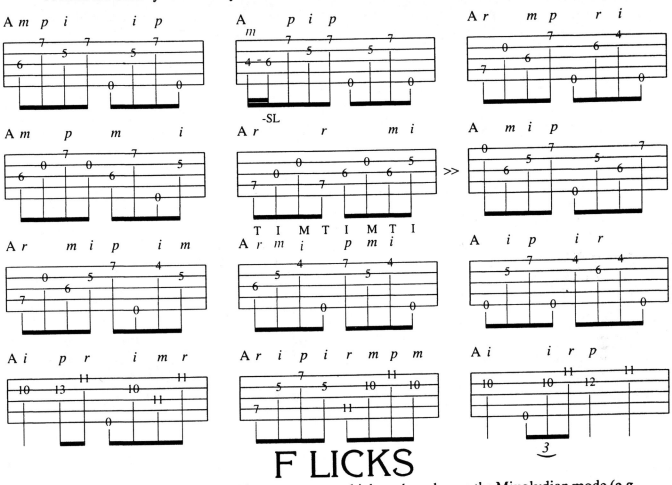

F LICKS

The F chord occurs in many bluegrass songs which are based upon the Mixolydian mode (e.g., "Salt River," "Little Maggie").

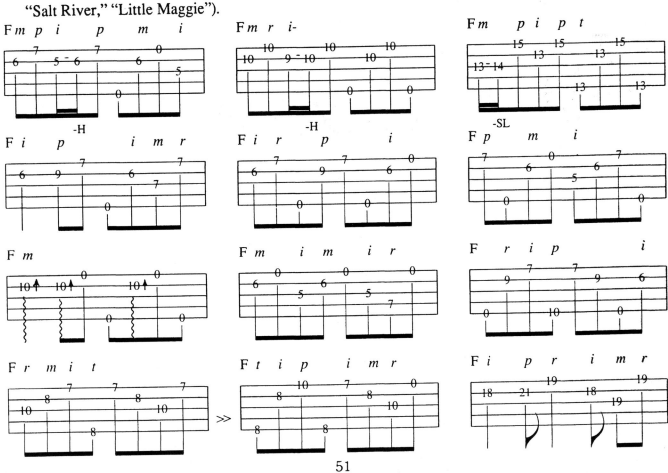

E LICKS

E-chord licks often occur in songs which follow the circle of 5ths, such as "Salty Dog" and "Don't Let the Deal Go Down." Play each F-chord lick 1 fret number lower, and you will have additional E-chord licks. Likewise, play each E-chord lick 1 fret number higher to have additional F-chord licks.

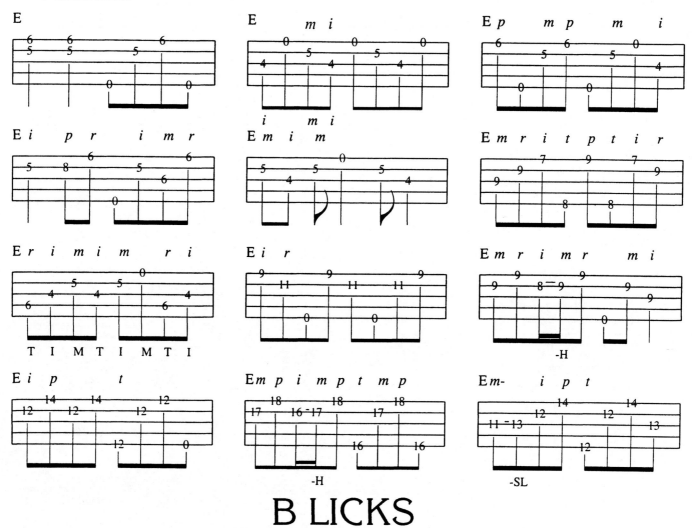

B LICKS

For additional B-chord licks, play each C-chord lick 1 fret number lower.

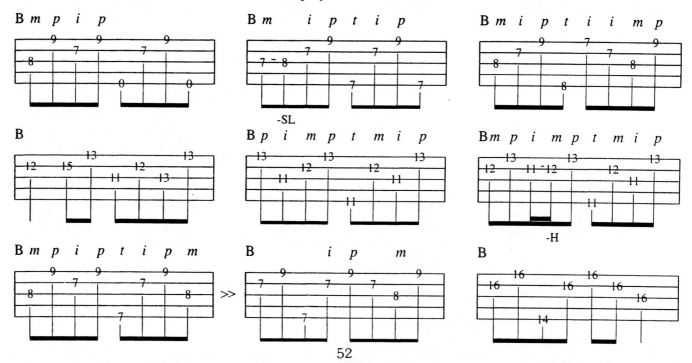

B♭ LICKS

B♭ licks can be found in any key. They are especially common in the key of F. A-chord licks which are played 1 fret number higher become B♭-chord licks. B♭ licks are also A♯ licks. (These are enharmonic — the same — chords.)

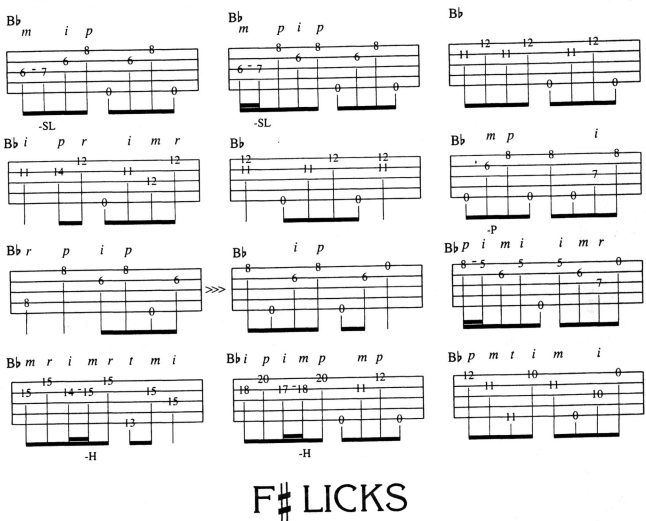

F♯ LICKS

F♯ licks often occur in the key of B. They also often occur between an F chord and a G chord. Additional F♯ licks can be played by moving the F-chord licks up 1 fret.

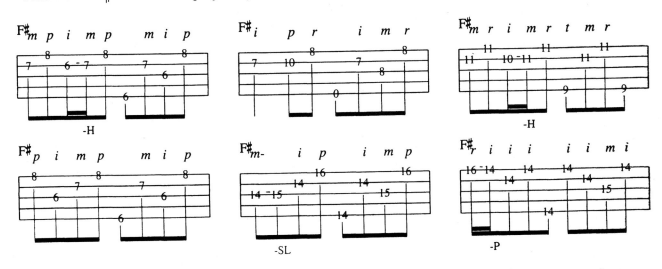

Note: For D♯ licks, move each D lick up 1 fret number. (These are also E♭ licks.) For C♯ licks, move each C lick up 1 fret number. (These are also D♭ licks.)

Am LICKS

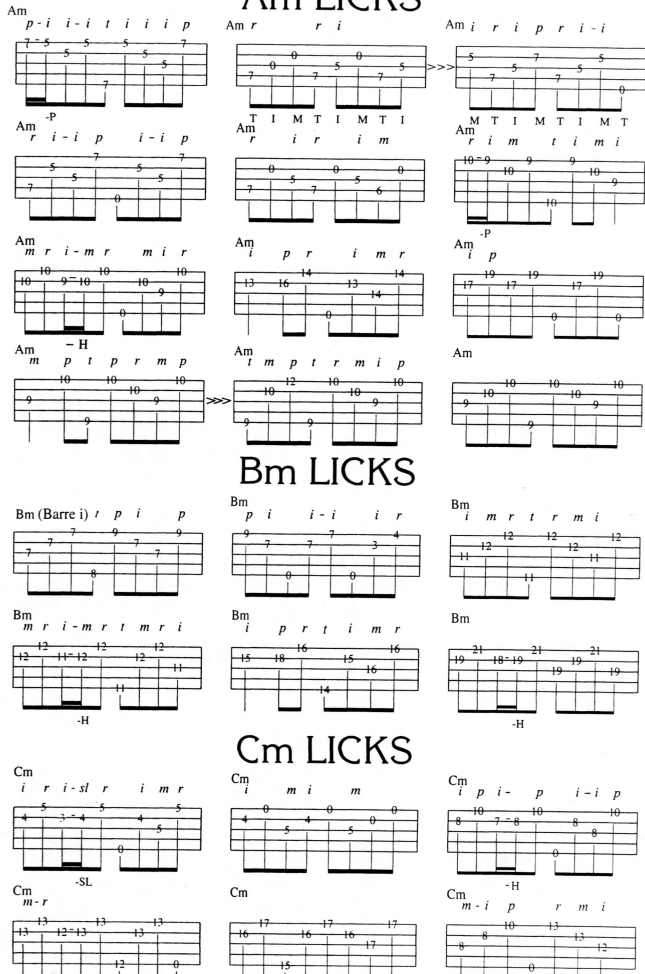

Bm LICKS

Cm LICKS

54

Em LICKS

Em licks are among the most frequently used up-the-neck licks for songs which are played in the key of G. Many of these licks also work as G-chord licks. Em is the relative minor of G; only one note differs between the two chords.

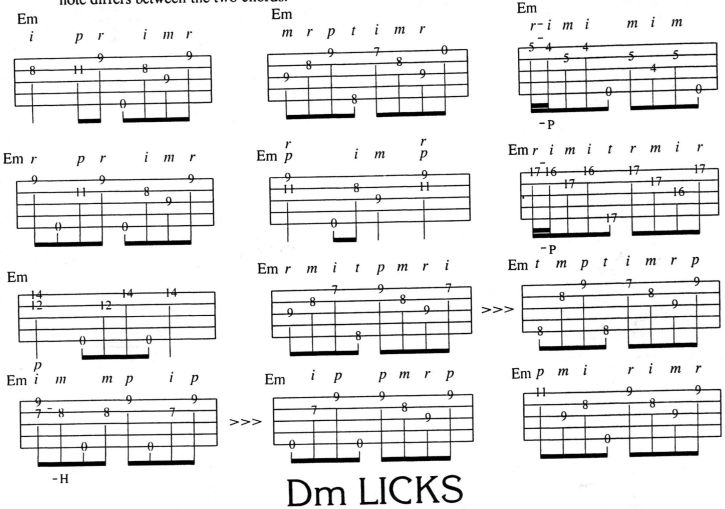

Dm LICKS

Dm licks also often work well against the G chord, especially before C. Notice that these licks resemble the Em licks but are played 2 frets lower.

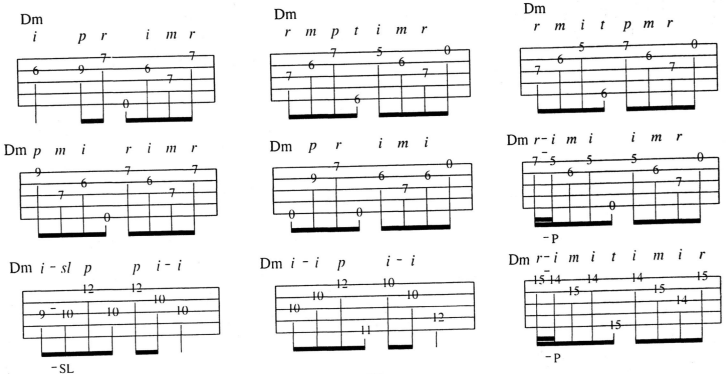

The following arrangement uses the same chord progression appearing on page 42 and can be used to play "Bugle Call Rag," "Dueling Banjos," the B part to "Hamilton County Breakdown," the final section of "Black Mountain Rag," etc.

This arrangement substitutes licks from pages 48–50 for the appropriate chords into the same arrangement that appeared before (page 42).

Notice, also, that it is effective to combine up-the-neck licks with down-the-neck licks using high and low tones. This also "looks" good to the audience, and sounds difficult.

Note: The final G-chord lick often moves down through the open first string at the end, to take the music into the open-string area for the next break (or back-up).

Chord Progression #1

• *Using licks from pages 48–50 for each chord.*

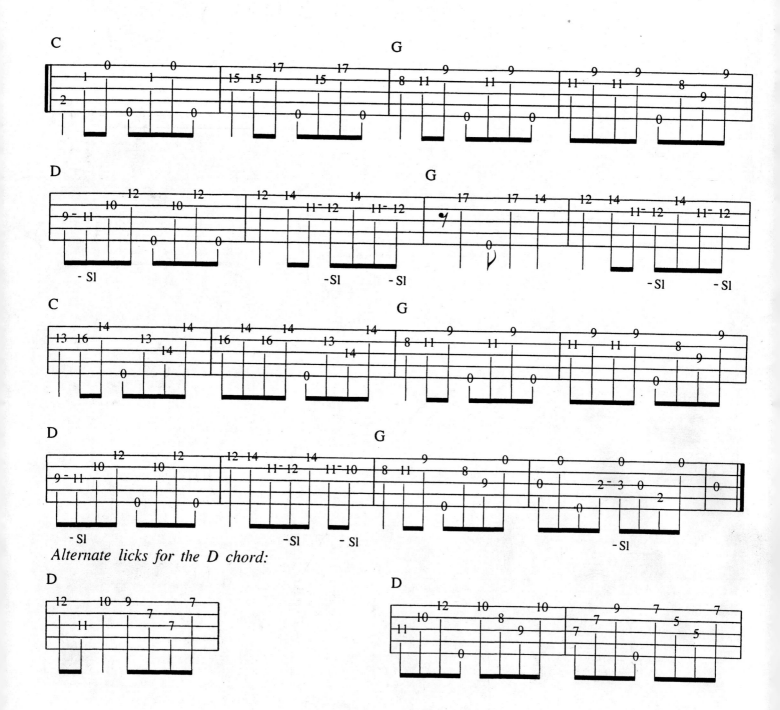

Alternate licks for the D chord:

The following chord progression can be used for an up-the-neck break for "Shucking the Corn" or any other song using these chords in this order. By playing the middle line twice before playing the last line, it can be used for "Lonesome Road Blues." (Compare this progression to "Lonesome Road Blues," page 44. Also see page 43.)

To have an arrangement for "Foggy Mountain Breakdown," substitute Em licks for the C-chord licks in the middle line and play this line twice before the last line.

Note: Read through this again! This is an important point for developing the ability to improvise up the neck.

Chord Progression #2

- *Using licks which employ the "CH" for the G chord.*
- *Note: "CH↓" is common for the final "CH" in a series. (Bend the string before picking it; pick it and then straighten it to sound the tone.)*

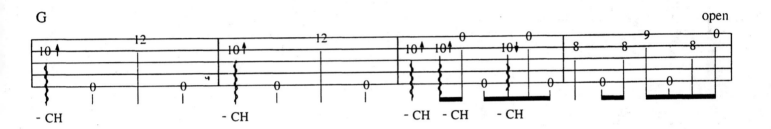

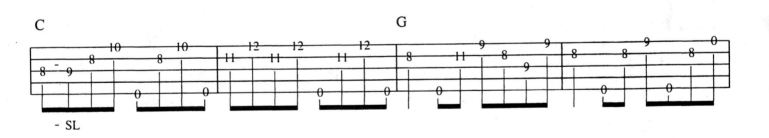

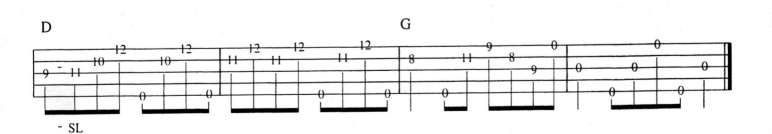

Chord Progression #3

- *Substituting different licks for the C chord (2 measures).*
- *Substituting different licks for the D chord (2 measures).*

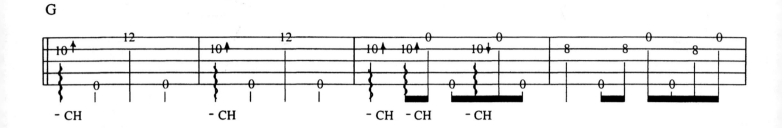

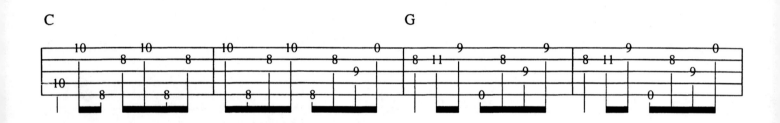

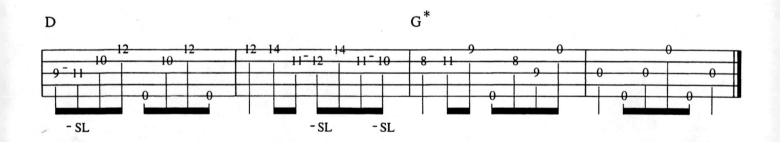

ENDING — OPTIONAL

- *To end the song, play the following for the final G chord in the above arrangement.*

The following arrangement is a fairly common way to play "Lonesome Road Blues." Compare this arrangement, measure by measure, to the one on page 44. Notice which licks are different. Then add the new ones to your collection of licks.

Lonesome Road Blues

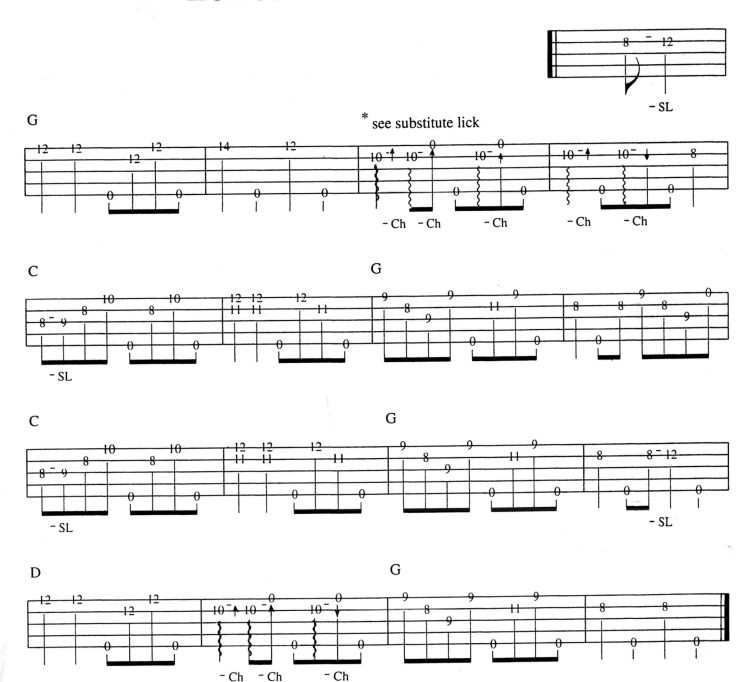

SUBSTITUTE (ALTERNATE) LICK
• *Mixed-up roll pattern (backward with forward insert) and fretted fifth string add drive without actually speeding up.*

G * ALTERNATE LICK

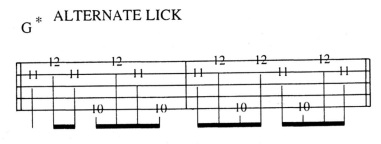

You don't have to change much to have an entirely different effect. See measures 3 and 4 (G chord) and measures 5 and 6 (C chord). The rest is like the arrangement on the previous page.

Lonesome Road Blues

- *Substituting different licks for measures 3–6.*

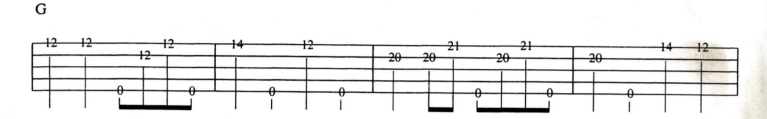

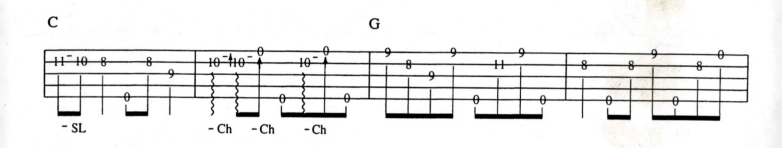

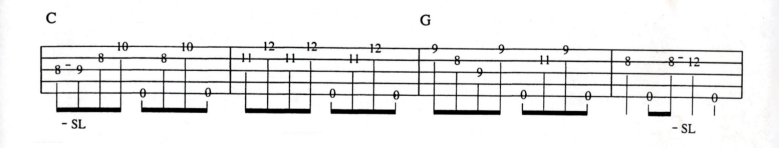

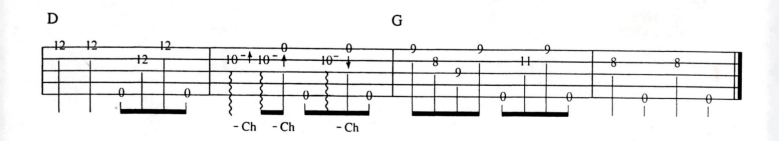

Notice that this arrangement of "Little Maggie" uses the "choke" for the F chord. This technique is effective for quite a few chords. Notice, also, that the F chord is played in the barre position. For practice, substitute different F-chord licks for these measures.

Little Maggie

- *Using the choke technique — bending the strings.*
- *Using different D-chord licks.*
- *Dropping through the open first string to the deep tones at the end.*

Intro or pick-up notes:

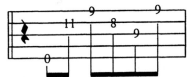

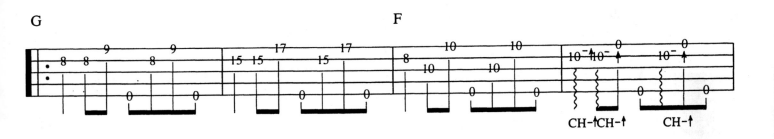

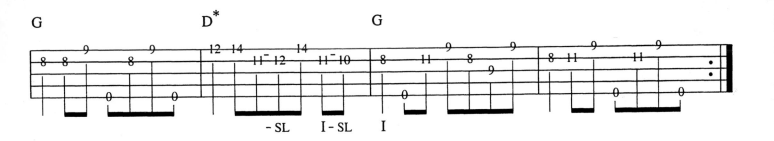

*Note: Substitute any of the following licks for the D chord in the above arrangement.

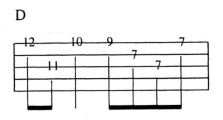

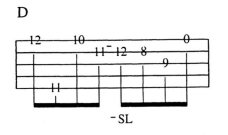

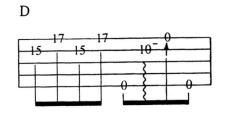

Notice the specific roll pattern or lick that is played for each chord in the following arrangement. The first 2 measures consist of the alternate forward roll pattern, which is played by the right hand while the left hand holds the partial chord position for the chord indicated by the chord symbol. The A lick in the 3rd measure is played with the left hand holding the Em (or "Cumberland Gap") position at the 10th and 11th frets. The pinky is used to reach the 13th fret. This is a very useful A lick.

Notice, also, that the chord progression works along the circle of 5ths. Compare the progression below with the chord progression for "Don't Let the Deal Go Down." Many of the same rolls and licks can be interchanged between these two songs.

Salty Dog Blues

- *With common up-the-neck licks.*

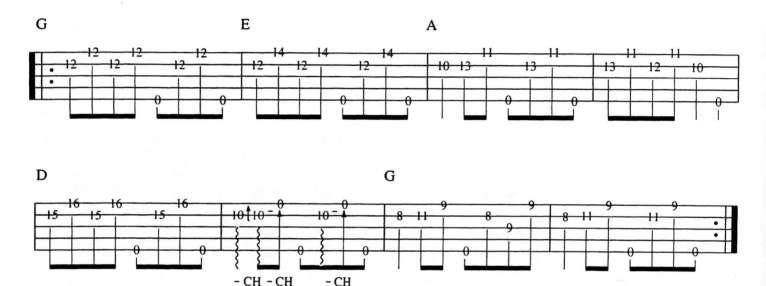

Salty Dog Blues

- *Using quarter notes for emphasis.*

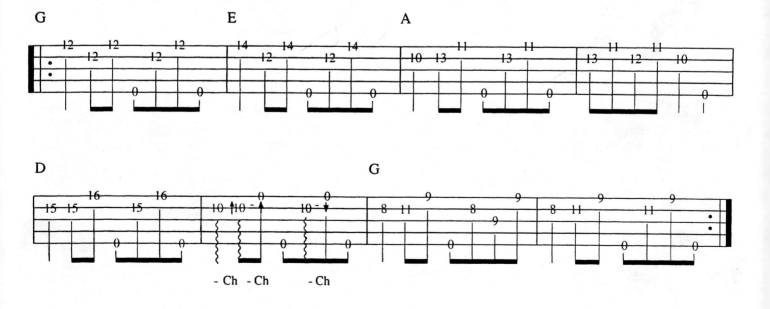

62

The following arrangement can be played for "Roll in My Sweet Baby's Arms," "New River Train," "She'll Be Coming Around the Mountain," and "Mama Don't Allow." It is comprised of licks which subtly imply the melody. However, these can also be interchanged with other licks for the same chords.

Roll in My Sweet Baby's Arms

• *Using licks for each chord.*

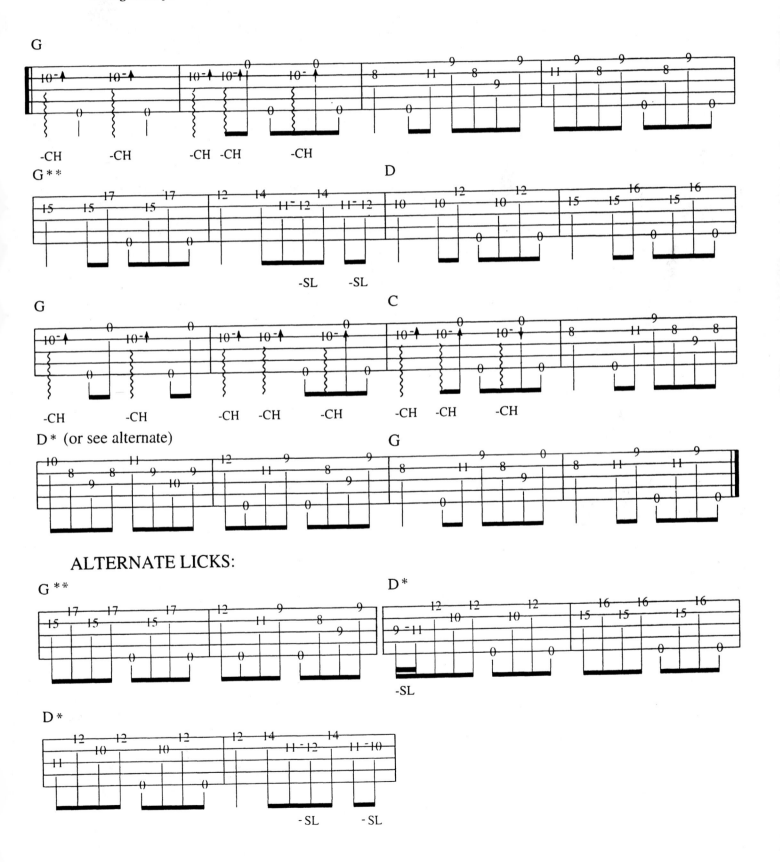

ALTERNATE LICKS:

Jesse James

• *Using licks and roll patterns.*

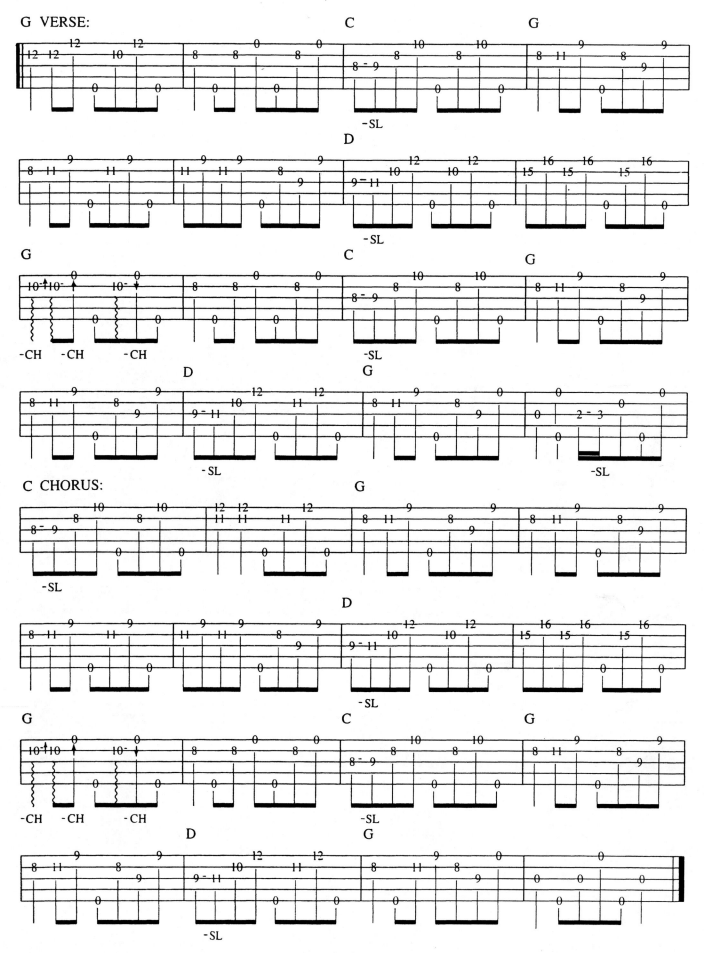

SUMMARY
LICKS

The following guidelines may help when determining which licks to choose, either when working out an entire arrangement for a song, or when simply substituting one lick for another in a song you already play.

1. Licks are played only for specific chords. In the following examples, a. cannot be played for b. because these licks do not work for the same chord:

a. G-CHORD LICK:

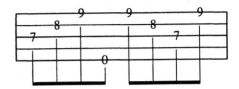

b. C-CHORD LICK:

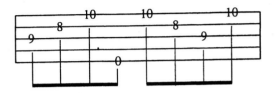

2. Licks can easily be interchanged as long as they apply to the same chord. For example, in the following, a. can be substituted for b. in any song:

a. G-CHORD LICK:

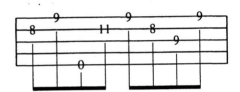

b. G-CHORD LICK:

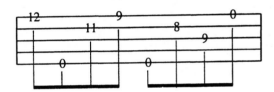

Note: The first note of the lick frequently functions as a melody note. If the melody note for the song is on the 8th fret of the second string (G), many licks which begin with this note will work in the song where that note is to be sung or played.

3. The rhythm for a lick can be varied in many different ways. Experiment to find the way you prefer the lick to sound. Remember, there should be eight beats in each measure or lick, regardless of how many notes are actually played. If only seven notes are played, you should pause (use a rest) after one of the notes in order to allow for all eight beats. Otherwise, your timing will be off.

A lick which plays all eight notes generally adds "drive" to a song. Replacing one (or more) of the eight notes with a pause (rest) adds emphasis.

a. G-CHORD LICK:
   (using all 8 notes)

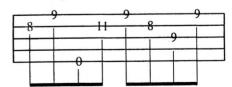

b. G-CHORD LICK:
   (replacing one note with a rest (x))

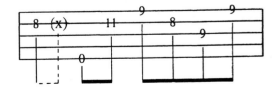

Note: If you are just beginning to work on your improvisational skills, don't worry about changing rhythm or working with the function of the specific licks. At this time, concentrate primarily on learning which licks apply to which chords. You can work out an entire song using any combination of the licks contained in the examples. Learn to use the licks according to the chords for a song first, for this is essential! The next step will be to find licks which will carry the tune for the song.

INCORPORATING
THE MELODY

On page 6, in the introductory section of this book, I mentioned that there are two basic types of up-the-neck arrangements: 1) arrangements which include the melody, and 2) arrangements which deviate from the basic melody (comprised primarily of licks).

The *melody* for a song is simply the *tune* for the song. Although there is ample freedom to deviate from the basic melody in an up-the-neck arrangement, particularly when it is played as a second variation, many songs have such a strong melody, you may find that you would like to incorporate the tune into your arrangements for those songs. Vocals (songs which are sung) frequently fall within this category.

An arrangement with a strong sense of melody is generally based upon *roll patterns,* where one finger of the right hand is used to pick the melody notes, while the other two right-hand fingers play background notes according to the chords for the song.

The first step in working out an up-the-neck arrangement which includes the melody is to pick out the melody notes on the banjo in the up-the-neck area of the fingerboard. Generally, these notes can be found along one string (e.g., the second string). The roll patterns can then be added, using one finger to pick the melody notes, while the other two fingers complete the right-hand pattern. The left hand will locate the necessary chord in the position which (usually) includes the melody note. Licks can then be played at the end of each phrase to fill in the spaces (e.g., where the vocalist might take a breath).

Note: Licks can also be chosen which contain the melody. Although the melody will not be as prevalent as with the roll patterns, the tune can be suggested by choosing licks which contain the most noticeable melody notes in the song. Generally, the first note of the lick is a melody note.

LOCATING MELODY NOTES ON THE FINGERBOARD

The following diagram shows the fingerboard location for each of the notes commonly used to play songs in the key of G. Once you have found a melody note on one string, you can use this chart to find the same note on a different string.

Note: I usually recommend finding the melody along the second string first, so that it will easily fit the forward roll or its alternate, by picking the melody note with the right index finger and playing harmony notes with the middle finger and thumb. This roll will place your melody notes rhythmically so that the song is in a *bluegrass context.* You can then move the notes to a different string if you prefer to use a different roll pattern, if you want to keep the left hand in one area of the fingerboard, or if the notes are located below the 5th fret and you want to move them up the neck. (The notes played on the fifth string are the same as the notes on the first string.)

```
—0——2——4——5——7——9——10——12——14——16——17——19——21——22—
—3——5——7——8——10——12——13——15——17——19——20——22————————
—7——9——11——12——14——16——17——19——21————————————————————
—12——14——16——17——19——21——22——————————————————————————
——————————0———————————————————————————————————————————
   D   E   F#   G   A   B   C   D   E   F#   G   A   B   C
```

HARMONY NOTES

A bluegrass arrangement for a song which contains a strong sense of the melody consists of two types of notes: 1) the notes which play the main tune to the song (*melody notes*) and 2) the background or *harmony notes*, which fill in around the *important* (melody) notes. Although the background notes are secondary, they are very important to the effectiveness of an arrangement. The harmony notes contribute to the color, the drive, the rhythm, and the overall tone of the arrangement.

Harmony notes are background notes which are supplied by the *chords* for the song. Play through the following as a chord progression and train your ear to hear these tones in harmony with one another. These are notes which can potentially be used for harmony when the melody note is played on the second string of the banjo. (The fifth string can be added to any of these combinations, for it acts as a drone in bluegrass arrangements.)

Note: Notice that the G scale is played up each string. Melody notes and harmony notes are derived from the G scale for songs which are played in the key of G. Each group of two notes forms a (partial) chord which can be used in the key of G.

HARMONY FOR MELODY NOTES PLAYED
ON THE SECOND STRING

Note: The harmony note is played on the first string. (There will also be times when you will prefer different harmony notes in a song.)

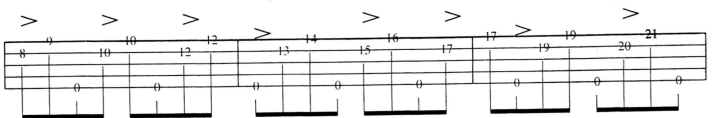

SEPARATING THE NOTES
(UP-THE-NECK USING THE FORWARD ROLL)

SEPARATING THE NOTES: (up-the-neck using the FORWARD ROLL)

Refer to the chord charts (page 138) for further reference. The harmony notes for any melody note can be found in the chord position which includes the melody note. For example, if you know the song calls for the G chord, find the G-chord position which either includes the melody note or is closest to it. You will often find that the melody note is a note within the chord position.

If you do not know the specific chord to play for the harmony, hold the melody note and play each of the three chord-position patterns (F, D, barre) which include the melody note as a chord tone; choose the chord that sounds the best for the background notes for that passage in the song.

For example:

Melody note: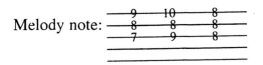

ACCENTUATING
THE MELODY

     Another important aspect for working out an arrangement is where to place the melody note(s) within a roll pattern. Each roll pattern has a distinct accent pattern which emphasizes specific notes. Usually, the finger which *begins* the pattern receives the most emphasis each time it picks the strings. Therefore, the melody notes should be placed so that they are picked by the finger which *begins* the roll pattern being used. (A melody note usually will begin the roll pattern.) Melody note = > .

FORWARD ROLL:

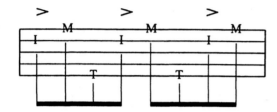

ALTERNATE FORWARD ROLL:

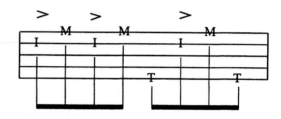

BACKWARD ROLL:

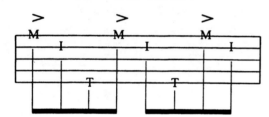

ALTERNATE BACKWARD ROLL:

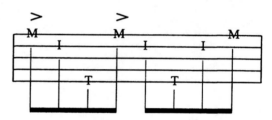

FORWARD-REVERSE ROLL:

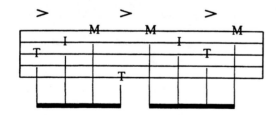

ALTERNATE FORWARD-REVERSE:

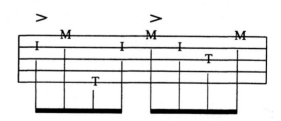

MIXED ROLL PATTERN:

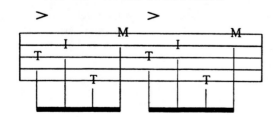

ALTERNATE MIXED ROLL:

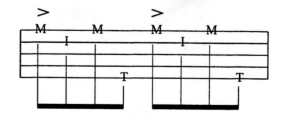

STEP-BY-STEP PROCEDURE FOR ARRANGING A SONG UP THE NECK:

1. Pick out the *melody* (tune) for the song with the index finger or with the thumb of your right hand. First, try to find the melody notes on the second string of the banjo. (The notes which are located from the 1st through 5th frets on that string can later be transferred to the third string on the 5th through 9th frets or to the fourth string on the 10th through 14th frets.)

2. Learn the *chords* for the song you want to play. Locate the positions for these chords in the up-the-neck area of the fingerboard. Note: The chords can be played as partial chords, rather than holding all four strings.

Worried Man Blues

- *Melody and chords only.*

G

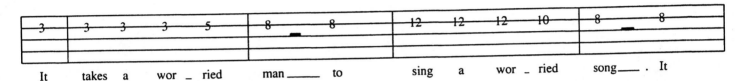

It   takes   a   wor – ried   man ____ to   sing   a   wor – ried   song ___ . It

C   G

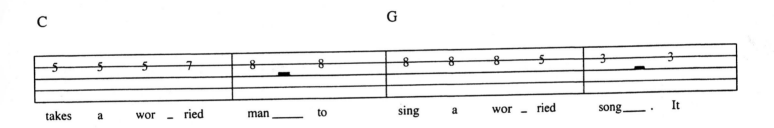

takes   a   wor – ried   man ____ to   sing   a   wor – ried   song ___ . It

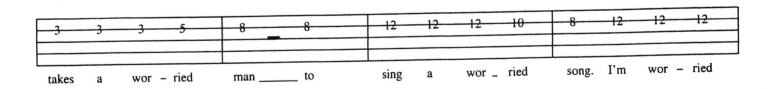

takes   a   wor – ried   man ____ to   sing   a   wor – ried   song. I'm   wor – ried

D   G

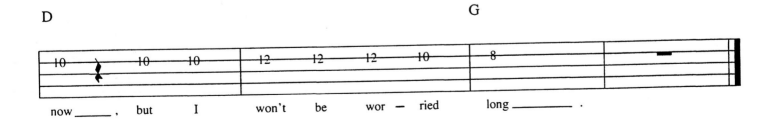

now ____ ,   but   I   won't   be   wor – ried   long _____ .

Note: There are eight counts in each measure of tablature (eight eighth notes).

69

3. Now, *fit the melody into the standard roll patterns*. When first learning to work out arrangements for songs, you should choose one roll pattern and try to use only that roll, repeating it over and over, playing the melody notes where they belong.

NOTES:

1. You can use any of the standard rolls as the primary roll for a song, but I have found that the *forward roll* (I M T I M T I M; T I M T I M T I) and the *alternate forward roll* (I M I M T I M T) best incorporate the "bluegrass" rhythm with the melody of the song when playing up the neck of the banjo. Therefore, I strongly suggest using one of these roll patterns as your primary roll pattern when first working out a song. However, if you find that it isn't working, try using a different standard roll as the primary pattern.

2. Try to locate the melody notes on the second and third strings in order to use the I̲ M T I̲ M T I̲ M pattern so that the right index finger will be picking the melody notes.

3. The left hand should be working from chord positions so that the right notes will be played as background or harmony notes around the melody notes, i.e., the 1st full measure below works from the G chord in the F position; the 2nd measure works from the G-chord D position. (Which position of the chord is determined by the location of the melody note(s).)

4. There will be a few places in every arrangement where the primary roll is awkward to play or doesn't sound good. Substitute a different standard roll or a lick in these areas. (This will be discussed later in more detail.)

Worried Man Blues

- *Adding the forward roll pattern.*

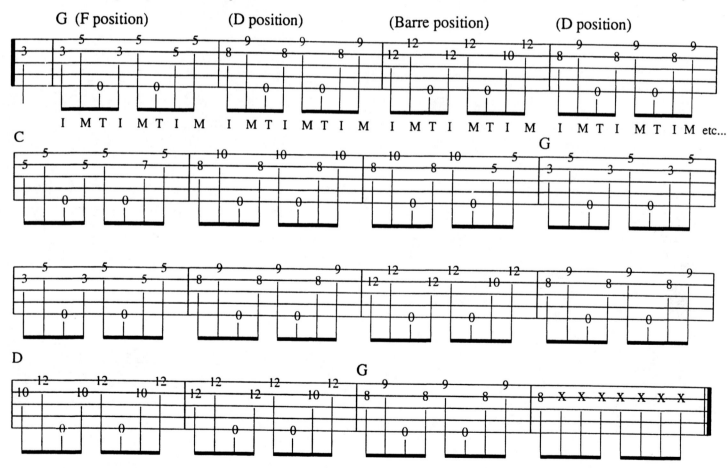

Note: When playing the forward roll, the right index finger picks the melody notes. Don't pause at the bar lines.

For practice: Substitute the *alternate forward roll pattern* for each measure, keeping the left hand on the indicated frets.

70

5. The following arrangement uses chord positions which are located in the same area of the fingerboard. The less you need to move your left hand, the easier your arrangement will be to play. Generally, it is not necessary to move the left hand drastically unless you simply want to, i.e., for effect (looks).

Note: Notice that the notes which were located in the previous arrangement on the second string below the 5th fret can now be played on the third and/or fourth strings by using chord positions which are located close to one another in the same area of the fingerboard.

Worried Man Blues

• *Using chord positions in one area of the fingerboard.*

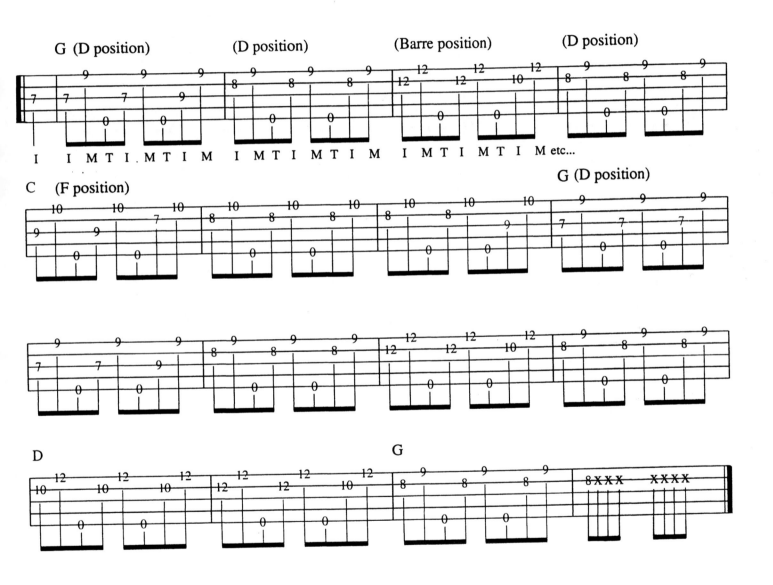

Note: Notice that the above arrangement builds upon the previous arrangement (Step 4). The right hand is playing the *forward roll pattern* in both of these arrangements, for each measure.

Again, remember that the *alternate forward roll pattern* will also work for each measure in the above arrangement with the right hand. (You are still playing the same notes, just in a different order, due to the order in which the right fingers pick the strings.)

6. *Substitute other standard roll patterns* in the areas where the primary roll is difficult to play or where the primary roll doesn't sound "right" to you. Remember, this is your arrangement! Anything will work as long as each measure has eight counts and as long as the chords you are playing with your left hand are correct.

The following example is based upon the previous examples, but it uses other roll patterns from the pages on the standard roll patterns (pages 9–12) in addition to the forward roll pattern.

Note: Remember to retain the basic structure of your arrangement. When one roll pattern is omitted, another pattern of equal length must replace it.

Worried Man Blues

• *Substituting other standard roll patterns.*

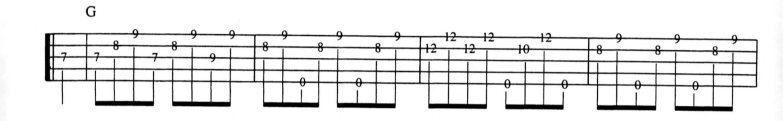

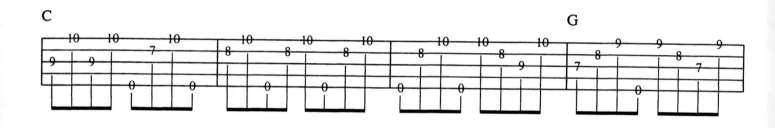

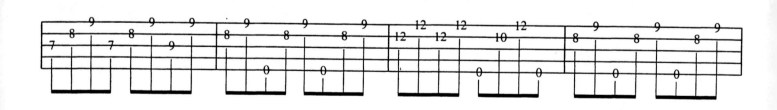

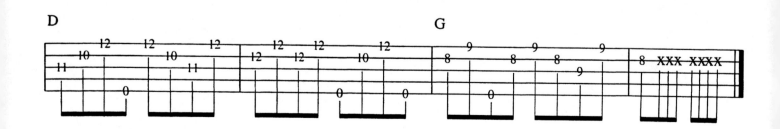

7. *Substitute fill-in licks* for the proper (corresponding) chord in any measure you prefer. Normally, licks are used to fill in the pauses at the end of the phrases where the vocalist might take a breath. Also, energy can be added to the close of the arrangement by using licks for the final D- and G-chord measures. In an up-the-neck arrangement, you can use as many licks as you like as long as they replace roll patterns of equal duration.

Worried Man Blues

• *Substituting licks.*

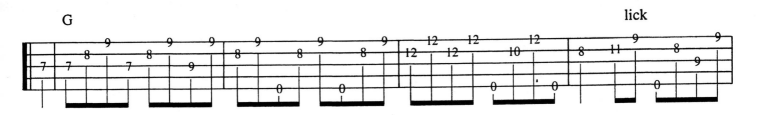

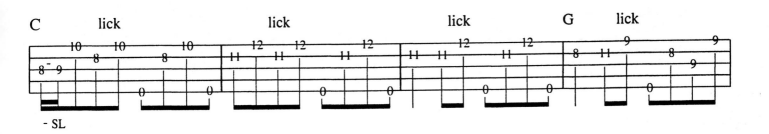

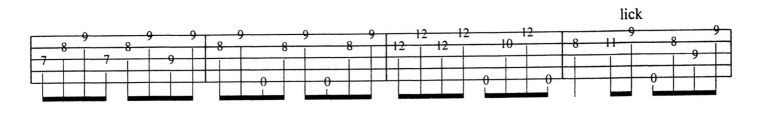

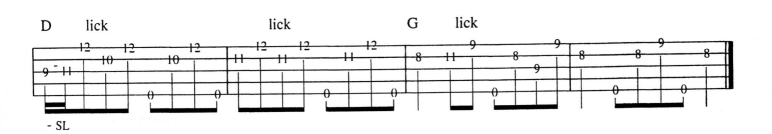

The songs "Red River Valley," "May I Sleep in Your Barn Tonight, Mister," "She'll Be Coming Around the Mountain," "Mama Don't Allow," "Roll in My Sweet Baby's Arms," and "New River Train" use the same chord progression. Therefore, the same up-the-neck break could technically be played for these tunes by combining licks according to the chords (e.g., 6 bars of G, 2 of D licks, etc.).

It is also true that some traditional tunes have the same melody but use different words. "Red River Valley" and "May I Sleep in Your Barn Tonight, Mister" provide an example of this. The same arrangement, with the melody, can be played for both of these tunes.

Red River Valley

- *The melody notes.*
- *The last line works from the D chord (F position).*

MELODY & CHORDS

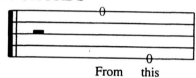

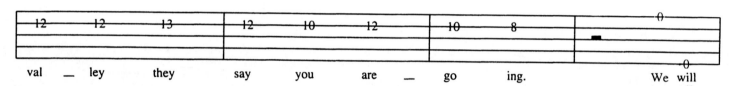

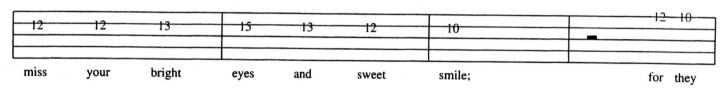

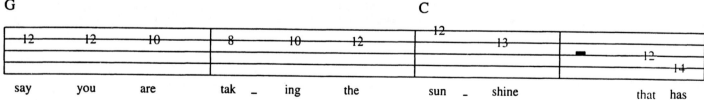

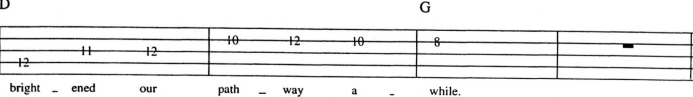

74

Each measure in the following arrangement contains a roll pattern which incorporates the melody. The melody notes are placed so they are picked by the finger which *begins* the pattern each time this finger takes its turn in the pattern.

When the forward roll pattern is used, the melody notes will be placed so that they will occur as the first, fourth, and seventh notes: I M T I M T I M.

1st   4th   7th

The above pattern is convenient when the melody is found along the second string, for the index finger is easily used to pick the melody notes. However, there may also be times when you feel it is better to play the melody notes on different strings.

The forward roll can still be used by beginning with a different finger, or you may prefer to use a different roll pattern.

Red River Valley

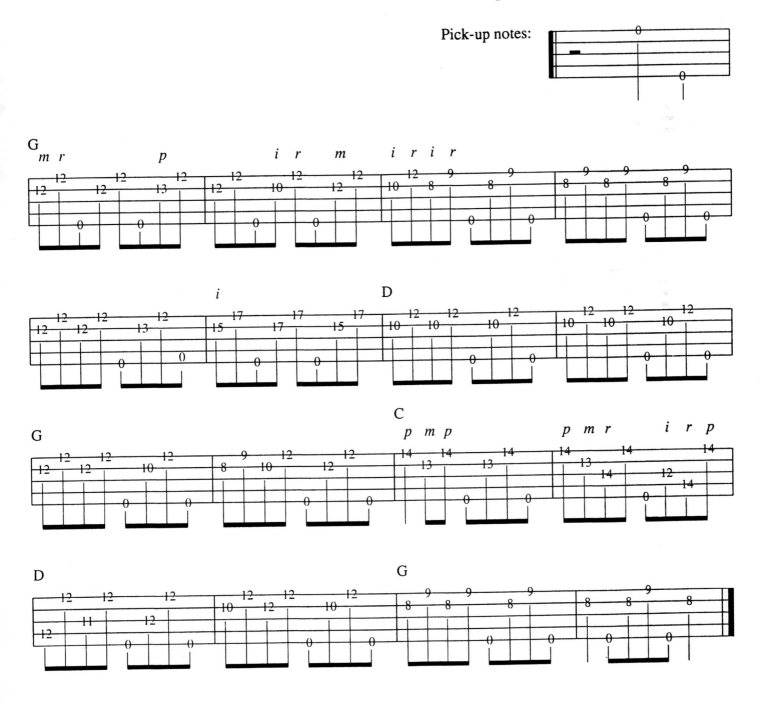

In addition to stressing the melody notes for a song through the natural accent pattern of the roll patterns, there are also additional techniques for bringing the melody to the front. The following arrangement works with rhythmic variety and with left-hand techniques in order to add emphasis to the melody notes.

Red River Valley

- *Using quarter notes (♩) to emphasize the melody. (Replace the next note which would ordinarily occur, with a rest or a pause.)*
- *Using left-hand techniques (SL, P, H) to emphasize the melody notes. (Slide to the melody note; pull off into or away from the melody note.)*

Pick-up notes:

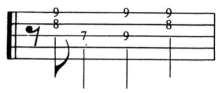

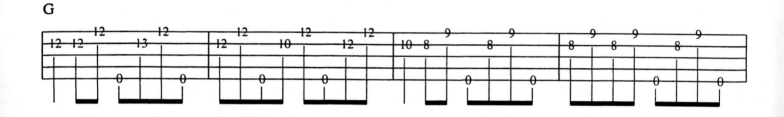

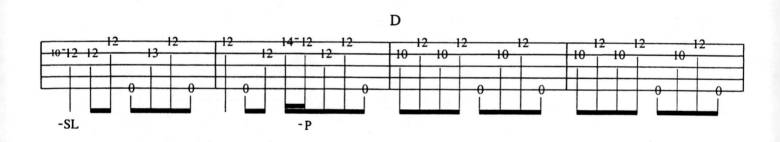

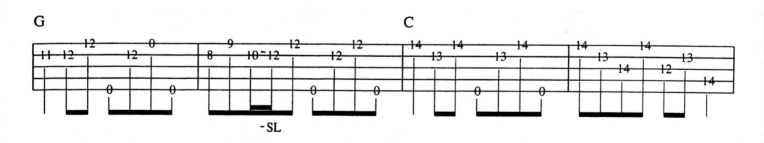

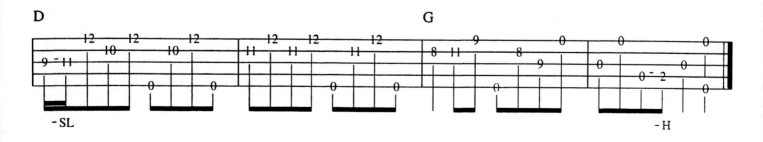

The arrangement below contains the melody notes for the tune "Hand Me Down My Walking Cane." Notice that these are played along the second string of the banjo. To form a three-finger style arrangement with the melody, play the forward roll pattern (I M T I M T I M) or the alternate pattern (I M I M T I M T) for each measure and place the melody notes so that they are picked by the index finger each time it occurs in the pattern. The middle finger and the thumb will automatically fill in with background notes.

Although you can play this by fretting only the melody notes with the left hand, you should eventually hold chord tones for the indicated chord so that they will provide the proper background notes to harmonize with the melody.

Find the position for the indicated chord which is the closest on the fingerboard to the melody note, e.g., G chord at the 12th fret for the first 2 measures; G chord at the 8th fret for the 3rd measure. You do not need to hold the full chord position unless you are picking all four strings.

Hand Me Down My Walking Cane

• *Melody and chords.*

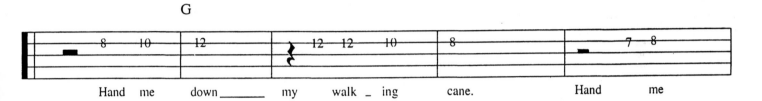

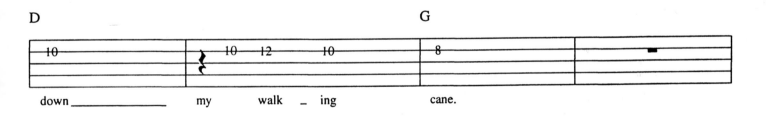

The following arrangement uses the *forward roll pattern* (I M T I M T I M) for each measure. Notice that the melody notes are played with the right *index* finger. Also, notice that the first note of each measure is usually a melody note.

Hand Me Down My Walking Cane

- *Incorporating the melody.*
- *Using the forward roll pattern for each measure.*
- *Playing the melody notes with the index finger.*

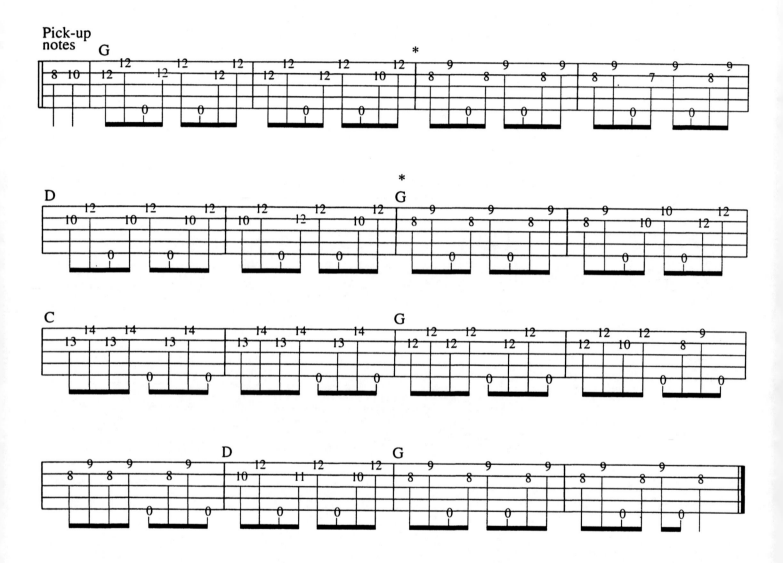

NOW: Substitute the following G lick for each measure indicated with "*."

Licks are frequently used to fill in the pause at the end of each phrase.

78

If you find that a particular lick or roll is a struggle to play in a certain place, or if you simply want to change something for your own reasons, do it! The fingering may be awkward, you may be tired of the same old lick, the "feel" may not be right, etc. You can substitute another lick or roll pattern, or create a pattern of your own, as long as you are working with the correct chord and the same number of beats or measures.

Hand Me Down My Walking Cane

- *Enhancing the arrangement.*
- *Substituting licks and alternate roll patterns.*

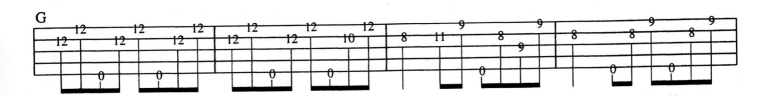

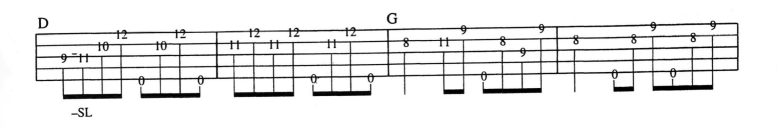

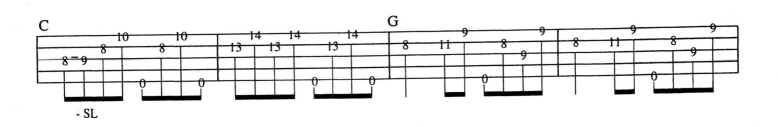

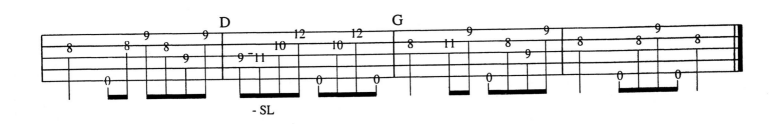

"Wreck of the Old 97" is a popular bluegrass standard. Technically, you could play the same rolls and licks for this tune as for "Red River Valley," for they follow the same chord progression. However, if the melody notes are included in the arrangements for these tunes, they seem quite different from one another.

Notice that the melody notes for this tune can be found within the chord position for each specific chord in this song, i.e., hold the G chord at the 12th fret (barre) to play the 1st measure, then move to the D position of the G chord at the 8th and 9th frets for the 2nd measure. Melody notes can usually be found around the chord positions.

Wreck of the Old 97

• *Melody and chords.*

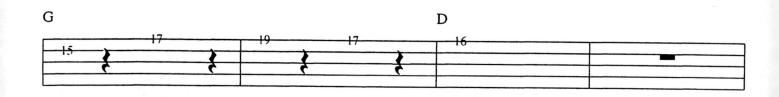

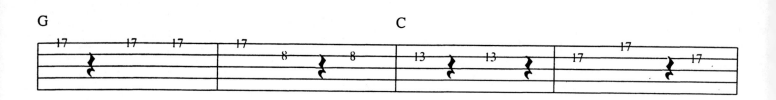

The following arrangement uses the *alternate forward roll pattern* (I M I M T I M T) for almost every measure. The melody notes are often emphasized by playing quarter notes (♩). Be certain you pause after each of these notes to keep the rhythm accurate.

Note: The *alternate forward roll* is extremely common for up-the-neck arrangements.

Wreck of the Old 97

- *Incorporating the melody.*
- *Using the alternate forward roll as the primary roll pattern.*
- *Emphasizing the melody notes in certain places with quarter notes.*

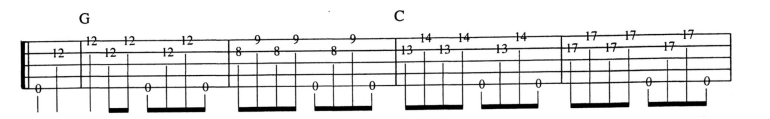

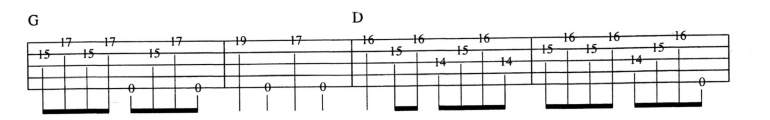

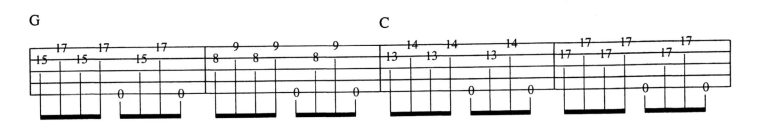

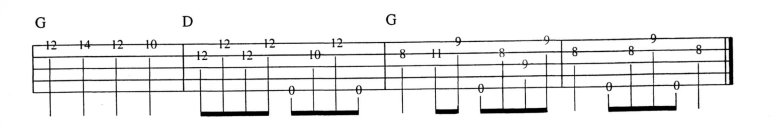

This arrangement substitutes standard up-the-neck licks for roll patterns in several places. This adds polish, energy, and interest to the overall effect.

Another technique is also included in this arrangement. The choke (CH) is a frequently used technique in up-the-neck arrangements. The 2nd measure of the last line below is actually an *up-the-neck lick* which can be substituted in any arrangement for the G, C, and/or D chords. (It works for all three chords.)

To play this technique properly: CH- ↑
1. Pick the string while fretting it on the 10th fret.
2. *Then bend* the string to raise the pitch.

OR when the arrow points down: CH- ↓
1. *Bend* the string first, before picking it.
2. *Then pick* the string while it is bent.
3. *Then straighten* the string, sounding this tone.

Wreck of the Old 97

- *Using standard licks.*
- *Introducing a new lick.*
- *Using the choke technique. (Two tones should be played with the choke — the straight tone and the bent tone.)*

Note: The open first string is often picked as the string is bent — at the same time.

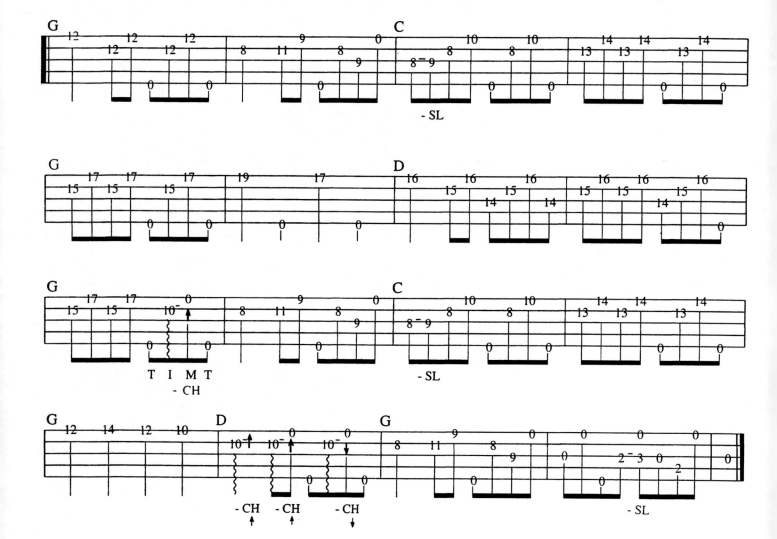

You can vary songs you already play by substituting different licks in your arrangements. This is an effective way to produce several arrangements for the same song.

It is also effective to combine up-the-neck licks with licks using the open strings. (Generally the final note of the up-the-neck lick will be an open string, in order to connect it tonally with the lower tones in the subsequent lick.)

Wreck of the Old 97

- *Substituting different licks.*
- *Connecting high tones with low tones (open string area).*

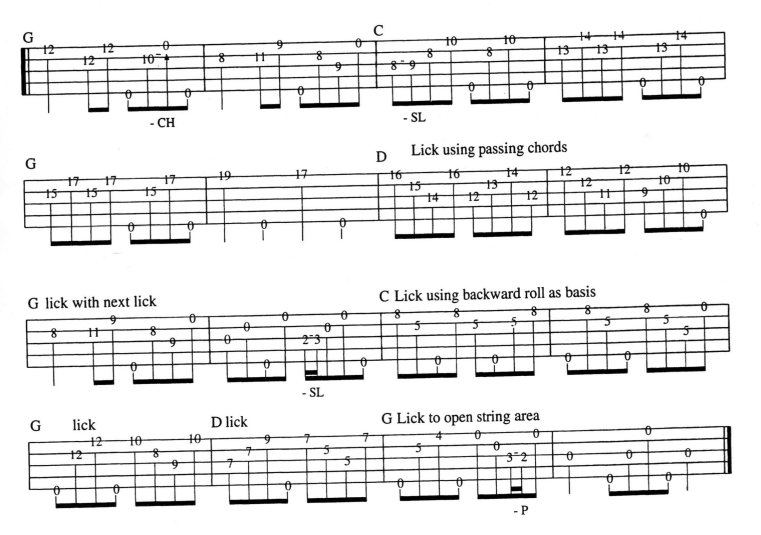

Substitute the following licks for the last line above:

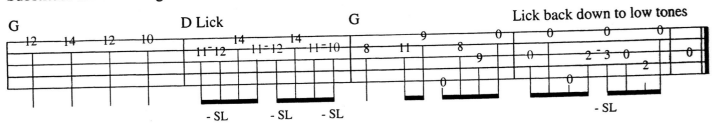

IMPROVISING
ADVANCED SECTION

The songs in the following section expand upon the techniques already covered in this book and also present additional, more advanced licks and techniques which can be used to embellish your arrangements. Each song is a lesson covering a specific technique which can be applied to other songs.

When working through each song, first notice the specific subject being exemplified. Then try to pick out specific licks and apply them to the chord progressions presented earlier in the book according to the proper chord. The more you are able to identify licks and utilize them in numerous songs, the sooner you will be able to improvise in any area of the fingerboard. Also, look for the techniques which have been covered so far.

In this section you will find:

1. Advanced licks and techniques for improvising.

2. Advanced uses for the X and Y positions.

3. Arrangements covering all areas of the fingerboard.

4. Advanced (altered) roll patterns.

5. Substitute chords and passing chords.

6. Use of the left thumb to fret the fifth string.

7. Melodic style.

8. Chromatic style.

9. Single-string licks and techniques.

10. Lead arrangements using back-up licks.

Plus: Endings.

Chord charts (major/minor/augmented/diminished/7th).

ADVANCED EXPRESSION
THE X OR THE Y POSITION?

Timbre is the formal musical term meaning tone quality. Tone quality is one of the elements or parameters which contributes to the effectiveness of a song. When first learning to play the banjo, you are taught to use the Y position every time you move up the neck in order to soften the tone quality of the banjo so that it is mellow rather than too bright. Although this is generally a rule of thumb for playing up the neck, as you become an experienced player and learn to listen to the "tone quality" of your music, you will find that varying the right-hand position on the head of the banjo can greatly enhance the overall expression for certain passages. The following guidelines may help you develop ideas for when to shift your right-hand position for expression.

When an entire arrangement is played up the neck, use both (X and Y) positions for contrast. The Y position should be used for emphasis, to accentuate certain areas. To use each of the following, move to the X position just before each situation, then:

1. Use the Y position for slides and chokes.

2. Use the Y position for 7th chords.

3. Use the Y position for secondary dominants (V/V chords), e.g., for the A chord in the key of G; for the D chord in the key of C. (Some people think of this as the II chord of the particular key in which the song is being played.)

4. Use the Y position to emphasize special licks.

5. Use the Y position when abruptly switching to a different area of the fingerboard.

6. Use the Y position for the last notes of an ending (up or down the neck).

7. Use the Y position if you move to the deep tones for only a short duration in a long up-the-neck break.

8. Use the Y position for Reno/Adcock-style single-string licks.

9. Use the Y position for an "echo" effect, e.g., the opening slide for "Lonesome Road Blues."

Summary: Use the Y position to vary the timbre of your banjo whenever you want to achieve a special effect. The more you experiment with this, the more natural this becomes.

CONNECTING LINKS
UP AND DOWN THE NECK

Once you are familiar with the up-the-neck area of the fingerboard, you can have fun working with all areas of the neck for the same song. This can be accomplished in several ways. For example:

1. Move up the neck for one lick only:

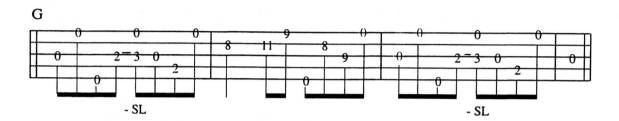

2. Play the A part down the neck (deep tones) and play the B part up the neck (high pitches), or vice versa.

3. Play only a phrase (4 measures) in a contrasting area.

4. Play an entire variation in one area of the fingerboard, and a subsequent variation in a different area for contrast.

There are several ways to smoothly travel from one area of the fingerboard to another. For example:

1. Abrupt change: Simply move your hand and play in the new area.

2. Use an open string for the last note of the lick just before the lick in the new fingerboard area.

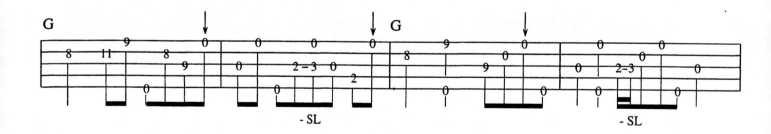

3. Connect chord tones with a slide, guiding the ear to the new fingerboard area.

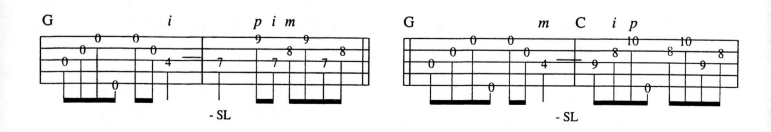

The following arrangement moves up and down the fingerboard, linking each area either through open strings or by sliding from a chord tone in one area to a chord tone in a different fingerboard area.

Compare the first two lines with the second two lines (variation). Notice that the left-hand positions are similar, although they are played 12 frets apart. It helps to keep in mind that the banjo fingerboard starts over at the 12th fret. (The C chord is held by the left hand at the 1st and 2nd frets and at the 13th and 14th frets, using the same position.)

Lost Indian

- *Linking the fingerboard areas with open strings.*
- *The key of C, using C, Am, and G as the primary chords.*
- *Using the mixed roll pattern as the primary roll.*
- *Using quarter notes for emphasis.*

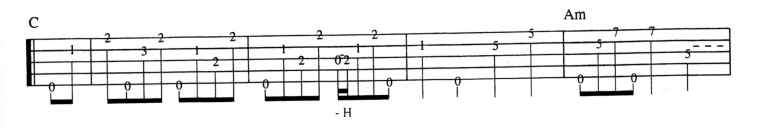

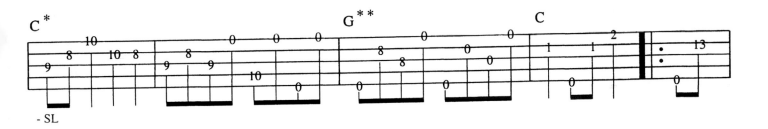

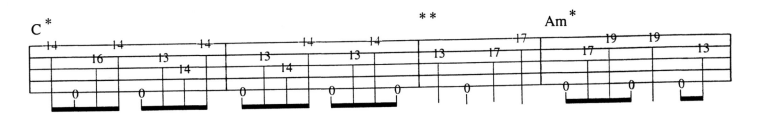

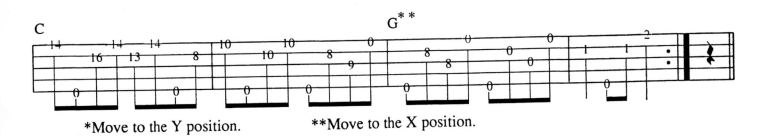

*Move to the Y position.   **Move to the X position.

This song includes two variations. The first (below) is played entirely from the open 5th-fret area. The second variation (next page) is played all over the fingerboard. For fun, substitute the *C-chord* licks from variation 2 for the C-chord measures in variation 1.

Sitting on Top of the World
Variation 1

• *Using the open-5th frets*

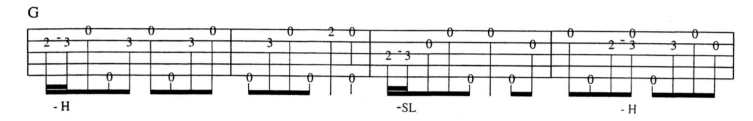

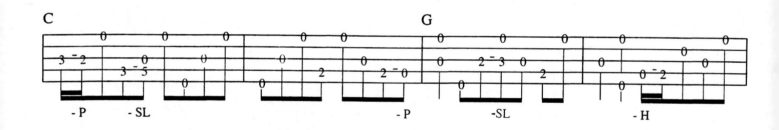

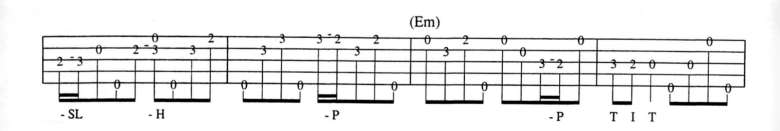

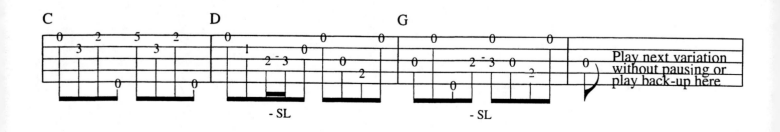

Sitting on Top of the World
Variation 2

- *Using the open-12th frets*

Pick-up notes:

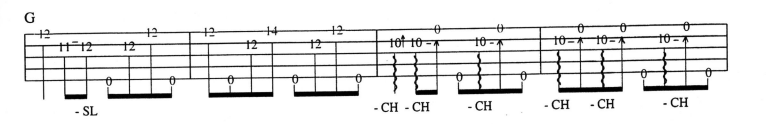

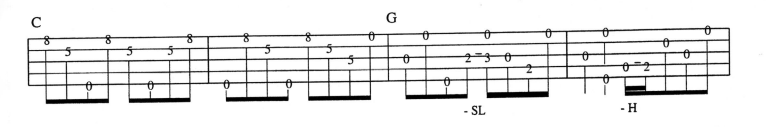

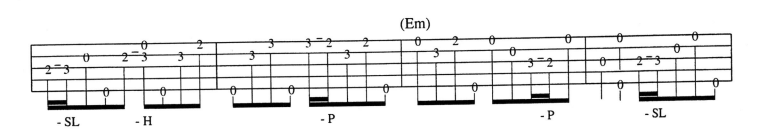

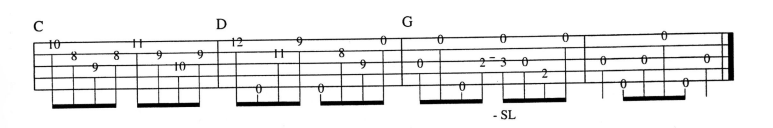

ALTERED ROLL PATTERNS

As you become comfortable playing and improvising with the standard Scruggs-style rolls and licks, you may feel that you have reached a plateau and wonder where to go from this point.

Many of the players in the 1990s have developed new roll patterns which are indicative of each individual player's style. Because the rolls still contain eight notes — one measure of music — the newer forms are essentially altered forms of the basic four roll patterns presented at the beginning of this book. These altered rolls can form the basis of an arrangement, or they can be used along with the more familiar standard roll patterns, playing them purposefully to add interest to a specific area of a song and therefore to the overall effect. Remember the discussion on drive, or the effect of each individual roll pattern? Note: Many of these altered rolls begin with some form of the backward roll.

Create your own eight-note roll and you will see that the effect of the roll can give a song an entirely different flavor. For example:

In "Blackberry Blossom" (p. 91), the basic roll is:

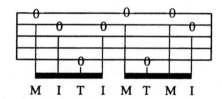

For "Wildwood Flower" (p. 92), the basic roll is:

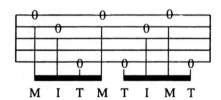

In "Sally Goodin'," each variation begins with a different string.

Additional ideas for altered rolls can be found in my book *The Banjo Handbook*.

The following arrangement of "Blackberry Blossom" uses a slightly different approach by altering the right-hand rolls. Notice that this song changes to a new chord every four notes (twice per measure) in Part A.

Blackberry Blossom

- *Using advanced licks and rolls.*

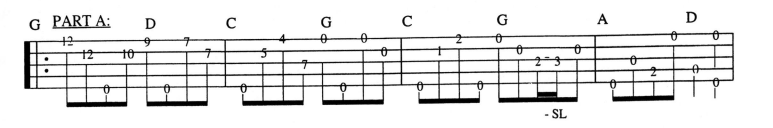

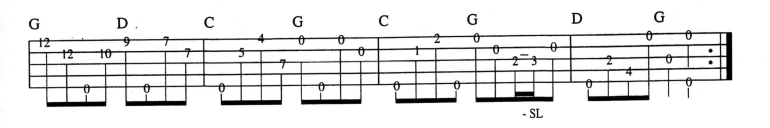

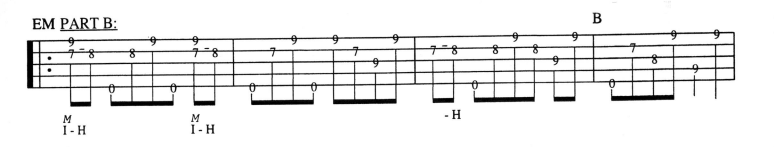

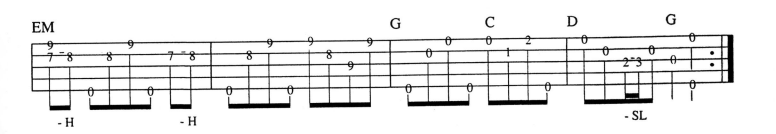

The following arrangement uses a roll-pattern variation which is often used by contemporary banjo players. This roll might be called the "reverse-forward" roll. Notice that it is the opposite of the forward-reverse roll.

Wildwood Flower
Variation 1

• *Melody notes on the first string.*

Key of G (G, C, D chords)

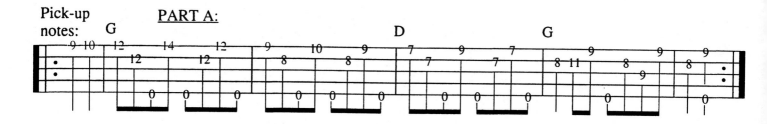

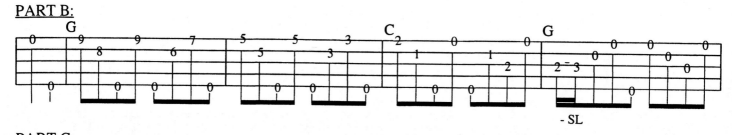

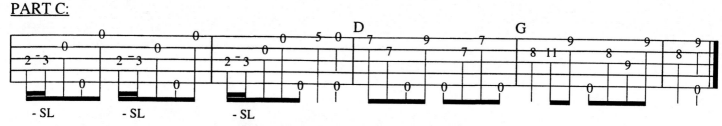

Wildwood Flower
Variation 2

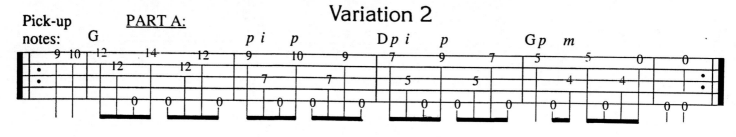

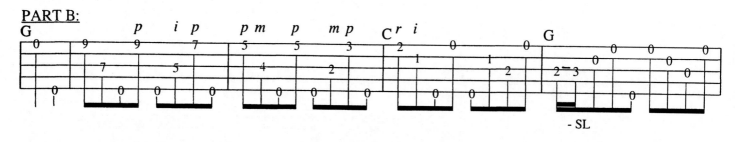

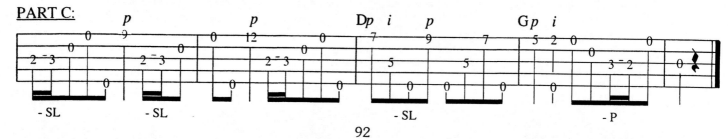

"Sally Goodin'" works primarily from the E-minor chord position with the left hand. Notice that this tune calls for the G chord for every measure except the fourth of each line. This tune can be varied many different ways.

Sally Goodin'
Variation 1

- *Using standard rolls and licks.*

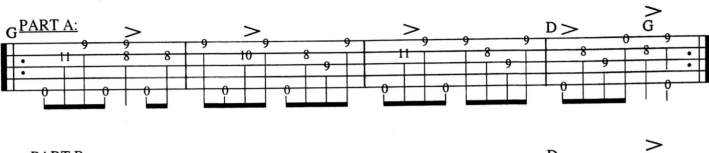

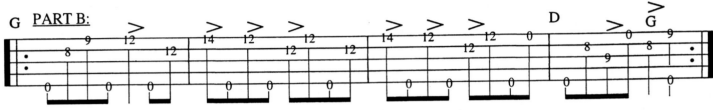

Variation 2

- *Emphasizing the first string — the middle finger.*

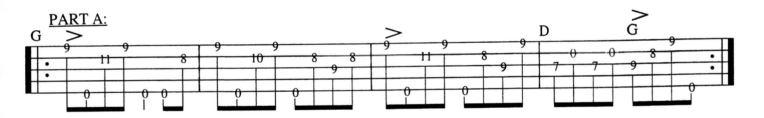

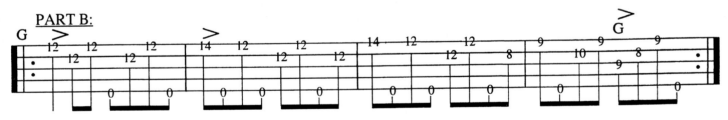

Variation 3

- *More motion — second string important for emphasis.*

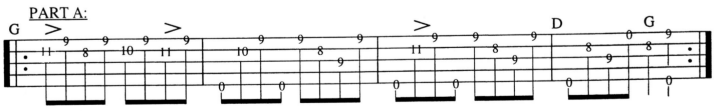

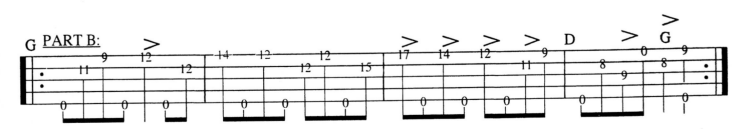

SECOND VARIATIONS

Each of the songs in this section contains two arrangements. I mentioned earlier in this book that many times, the second arrangement is played up the neck, while the first arrangement is played on the deeper tones of the banjo. However, some songs are often traditionally played primarily as up-the-neck arrangements... e.g., "Lonesome Road Blues" (Scruggs version), "Sally Ann," "Dear Old Dixie," and "Bugle Call Rag." You are not limited by this, of course, but it is fun to see how many different ways you can play one tune in the up-the-neck area of the fingerboard.

Amazingly, you do not have to change very much to create an entirely different-sounding second variation for a song. Compare the two versions for "Sally Ann." Only 3 measures are significantly different. (Remember the discussion on substituting licks where it was demonstrated that you can change only one lick in an arrangement for a song and have an entirely different variation, e.g., through choking the strings.)

However, you may want to change your entire style from basic bluegrass to one with melodic or chromatic (scale-tone) runs, which may necessitate changing more of the basic arrangement. Notice that the first two arrangements for "Don't Let the Deal Go Down" begin exactly alike, using the same E-chord rolls for the first 2 measures. However, with the A chord, the first variation uses traditional Scruggs-style licks, while the second arrangement uses more advanced melodic-style A-chord and D-chord licks. (Notice also that the third arrangement uses the left thumb to fret the fifth string, adding a neighboring scale tone to the basic chord in the roll, creating a Scruggs-style melodic/chromatic effect for the A and D chords.)

NOTES
1. Scruggs-style licks work primarily from chord positions with the left hand.
2. Melodic-style licks work with the diatonic scale line (page 100).
3. Chromatic-style licks work with the chromatic scale line (page 110).
4. Melodic and chromatic licks are developed by playing the notes from the scale line on different strings so that the right hand does not have to pick the same string twice in a row.

This arrangement introduces a lick which is often used to play many bluegrass songs. The lick occurring in the 3rd measure of lines 3, 4, and 5 involves playing the open second string, then sliding the left middle finger to the 7th fret, third string, then moving back into the E-minor position for the next measure.

Sally Ann
Variation 1

Traditional

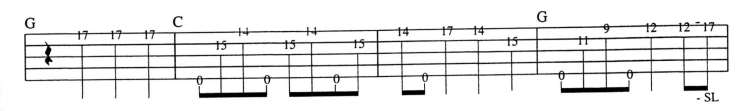

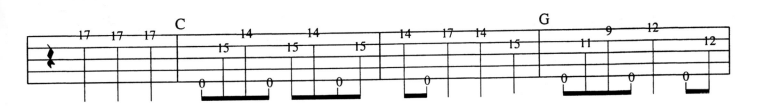

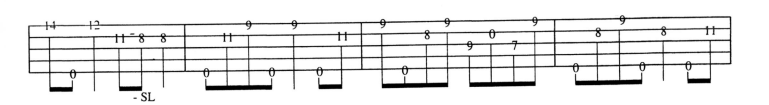

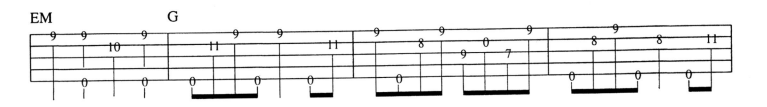

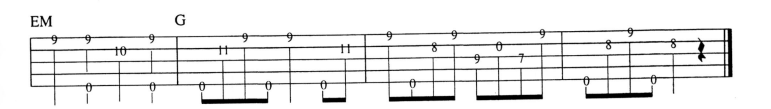

95

This arrangement sounds quite different from variation 1. However, only measures 6–9 are actually changed. Changing the licks in one phrase only can make a significant difference and results easily in a second variation.

Sally Ann
Variation 2

• *Using different licks in measures 6–9.*

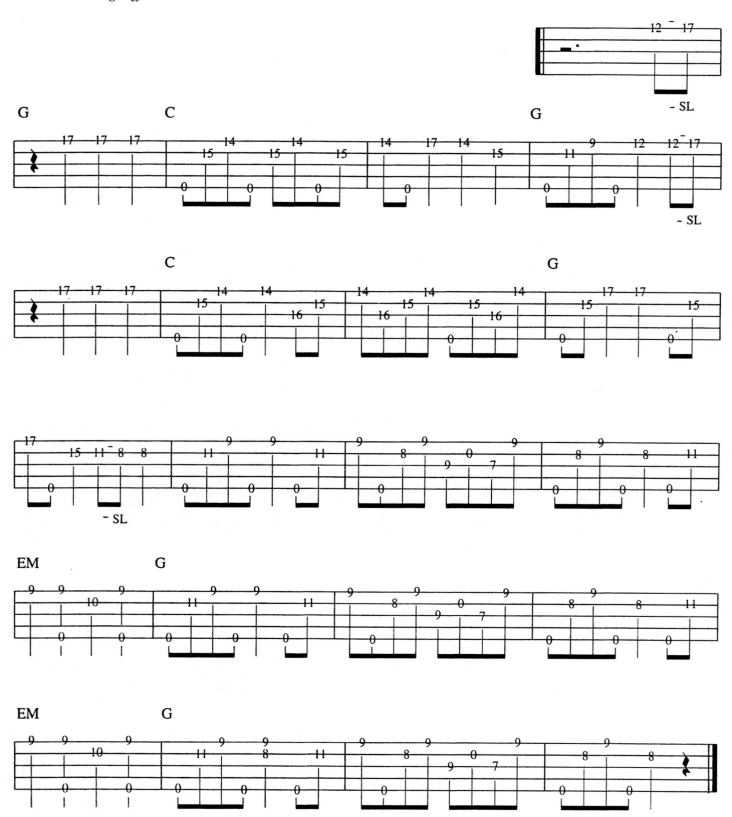

Compare each of the following arrangements, chord by chord. Notice which licks are interchanged for each chord. Then try using these licks for the same chord in other songs.

Don't Let the Deal Go Down

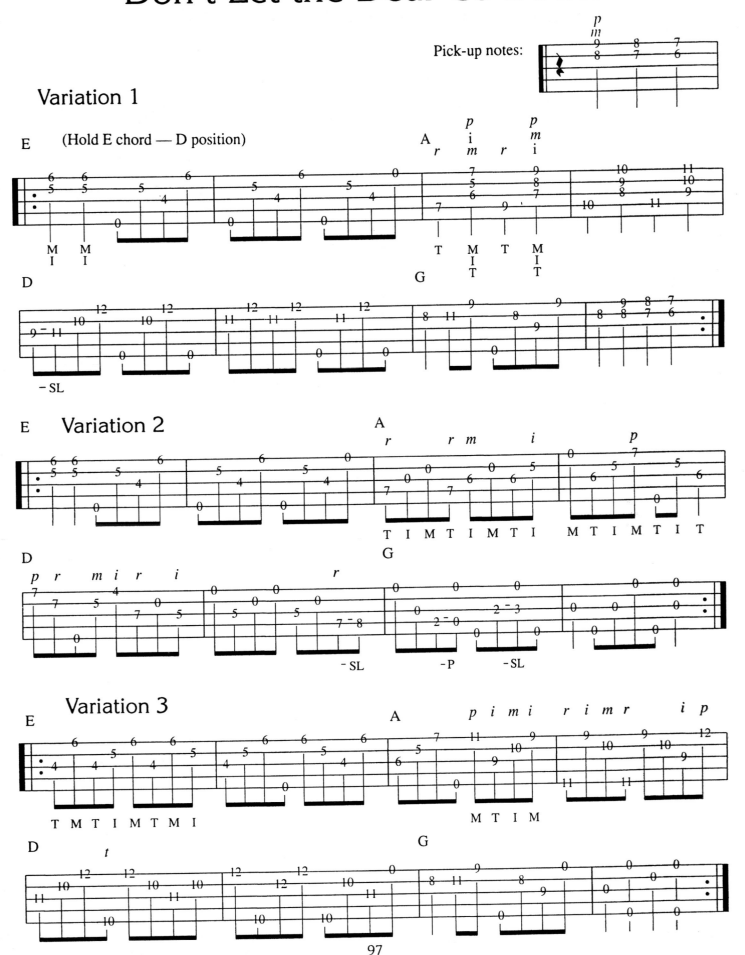

The alternate forward roll pattern is the basis for Part A. The forward-reverse roll is the basis for each measure in Part B. Part B also uses the thumb to fret the fifth string, adding color.

Look Down, Look Down
Variation 1

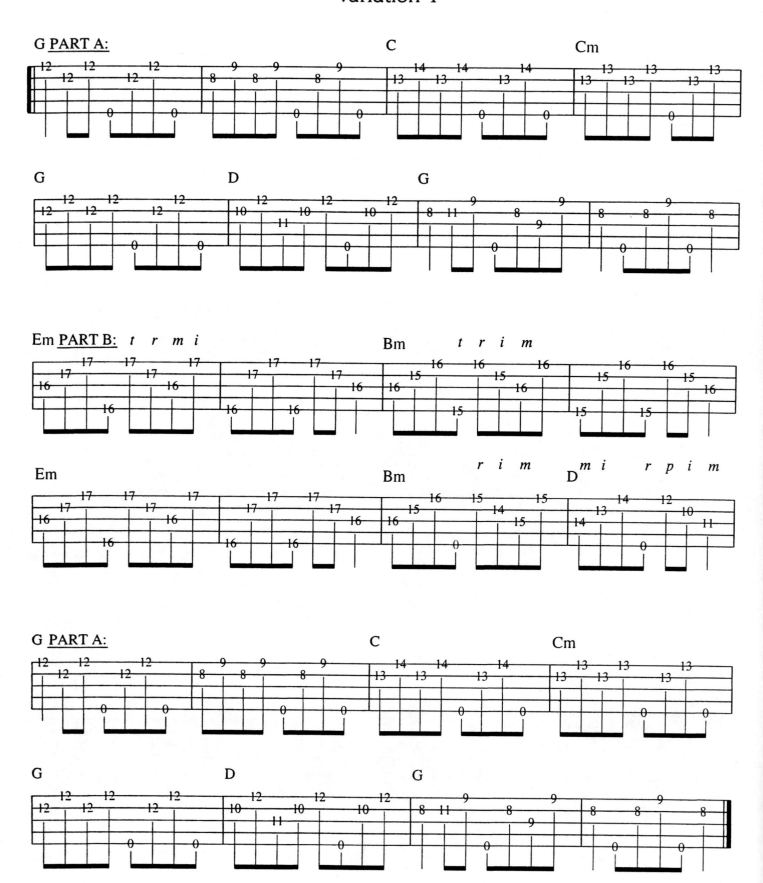

Compare the following variation measure by measure with variation 1 on the previous page. Notice that only a few notes are changed, yet the two arrangements sound like variations of one another, rather than like the same arrangement. Simply changing one note in a lick, or using the thumb to fret the fifth string instead of playing it open, can substantially change the overall result.

Look Down, Look Down
Variation 2

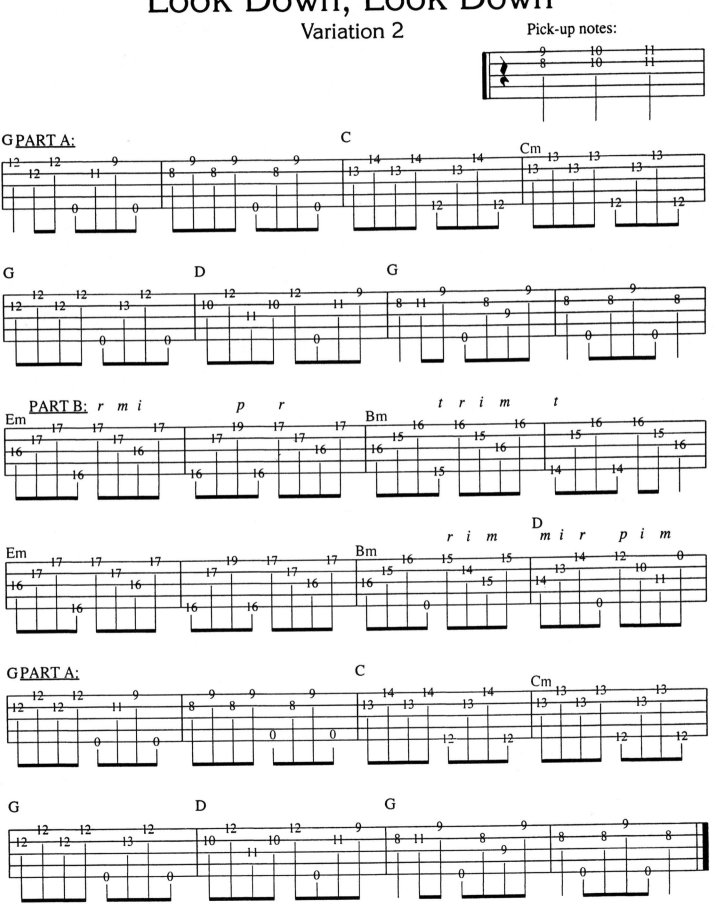

MELODIC LICKS

When *melodic-style* playing first became popularized in the 1960s, several terms were used to describe the style. The most common were a) *fiddle style,* because the banjo is played in the style of the fiddle, using fiddle-style licks, and many fiddle tunes are played in this style; b) *Keith style,* because Bill Keith was among the first banjo players to record in this style; and c) *melodic style,* because almost every note that is played is a melody note.

Melodic-style playing is based upon the diatonic scale, usually for the key in which the song is played. Many times complete arrangements are played in this style. However, melodic licks which are derived from the scale can also be used in standard bluegrass arrangements.

The diatonic scale uses an eight-tone pattern along one string.

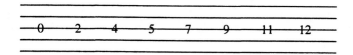

Frequently, melodic licks are drawn from a *circular diatonic scale:*

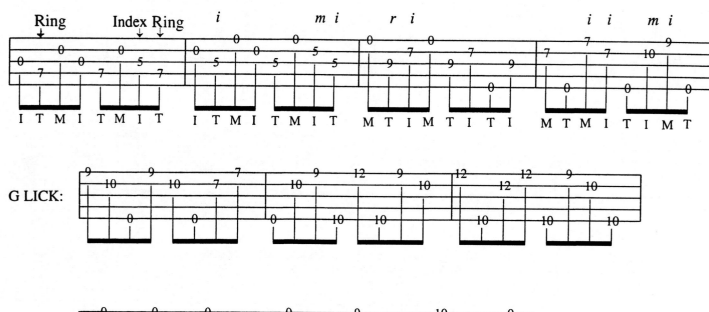

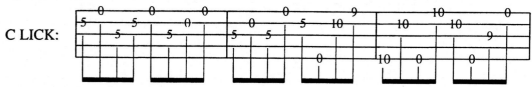

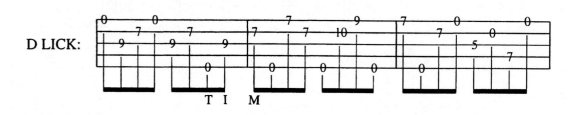

Note: Additional melodic and chromatic licks are covered in *Splitting the Licks.*

Dixie

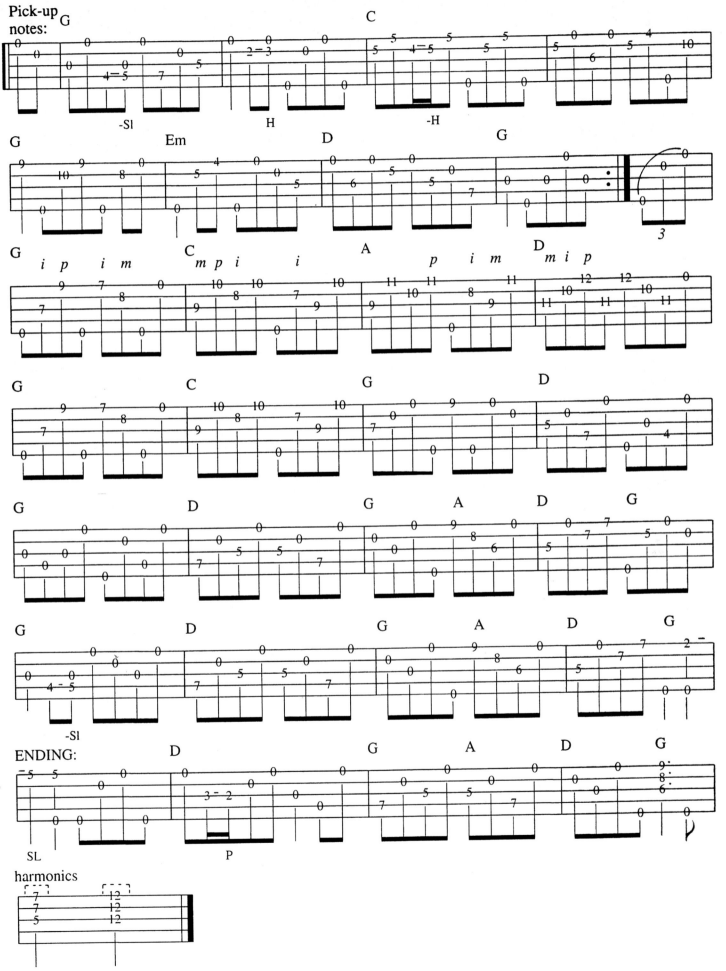

This is a fairly typical example of a fiddle tune which is played on the banjo in the melodic-style of playing. A triplet is often used to begin songs of this nature. Also, notice that it uses a combination of melodic licks which are based upon the G scale and three-finger roll patterns which are played for the G chord. Notice also that the tune calls for frequent chord changes. This is another common feature of many fiddle tunes. (Fiddle tunes seem to either stay on the same chord throughout most of the song without any change (e.g., "Gray Eagle" and "Sally Goodin'") or they call for a new chord at least once per measure (e.g., "Blackberry Blossom," "Cuckoo's Nest," and "Crazy Creek").

Cuckoo's Nest

• *In the melodic style of playing — based upon the G-major scale.*

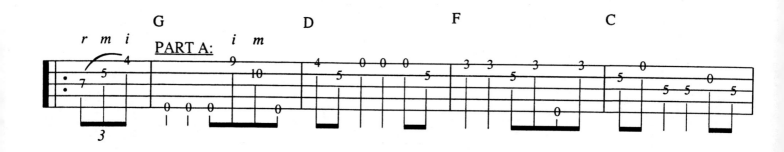

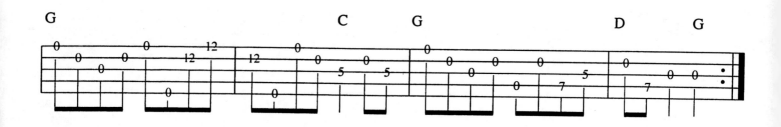

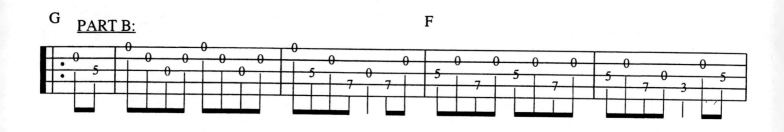

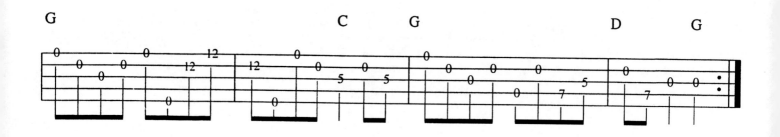

"Crazy Creek" is another example of a melodic-style arrangement for a fiddle tune calling for frequent chord changes, melodic-style licks in Part A, and right-hand roll patterns while holding chord positions with the left hand for Part B. The introduction below is also a standard way to begin fiddle tunes. This can effectively precede virtually any fiddle tune which is played in the key of G on the banjo. Fiddle tunes are also frequently divided into parts or sections. For this tune, play the intro twice, play Part A twice, play Part B once, then repeat Part A again (once). Also, place the capo on the 2nd fret to play this in the key of A.

Crazy Creek

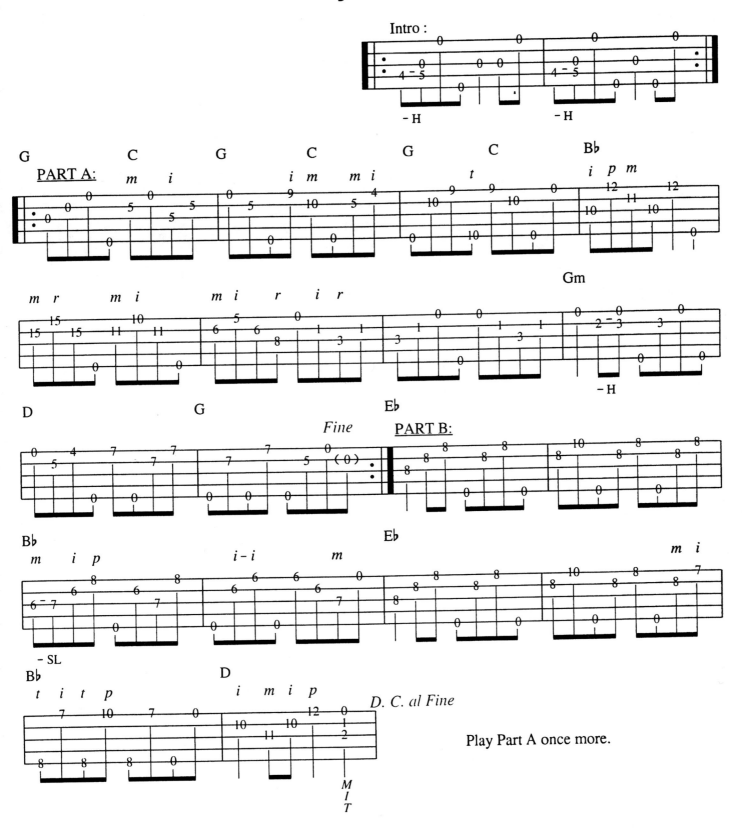

Play Part A once more.

I mentioned earlier that many melodic-style tunes begin with a triplet. The triplet is the main motif for Part A of this tune. (Play three notes in the same amount of time that two eighth notes are usually played: ♪♪♪ = ♪♪).

"Limerock" is divided into several sections, each section being played in a different key. (Each section is centered around a different set of chords — the banjo remains in G tuning.) All of the *parts* should be played in sequence *without stopping* between them. Normally, "Limerock" is played with the capo on the 2nd fret, which is common for many fiddle tunes which are played on the banjo.

Limerock

- *Play through each section twice.*
- *Substitute ending 2 for ending 1 the second time through.*

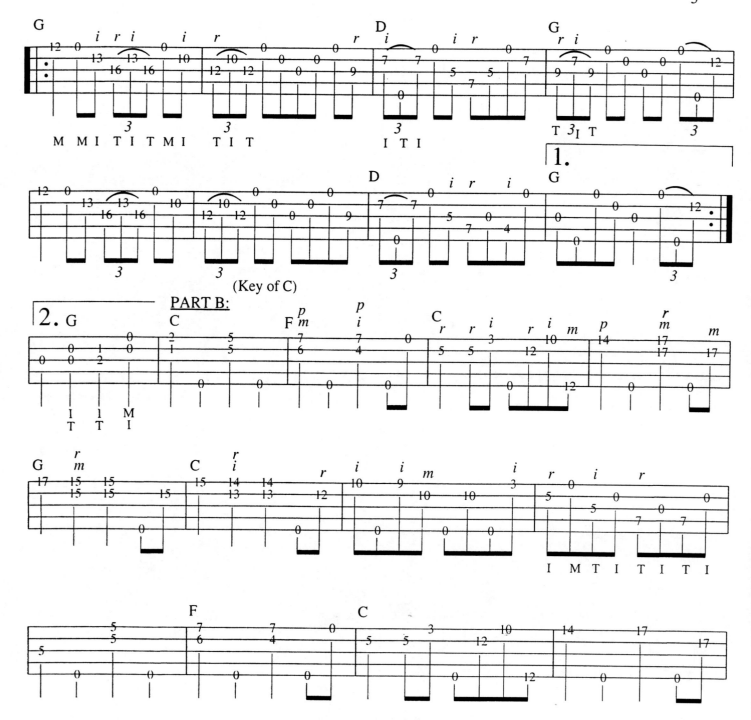

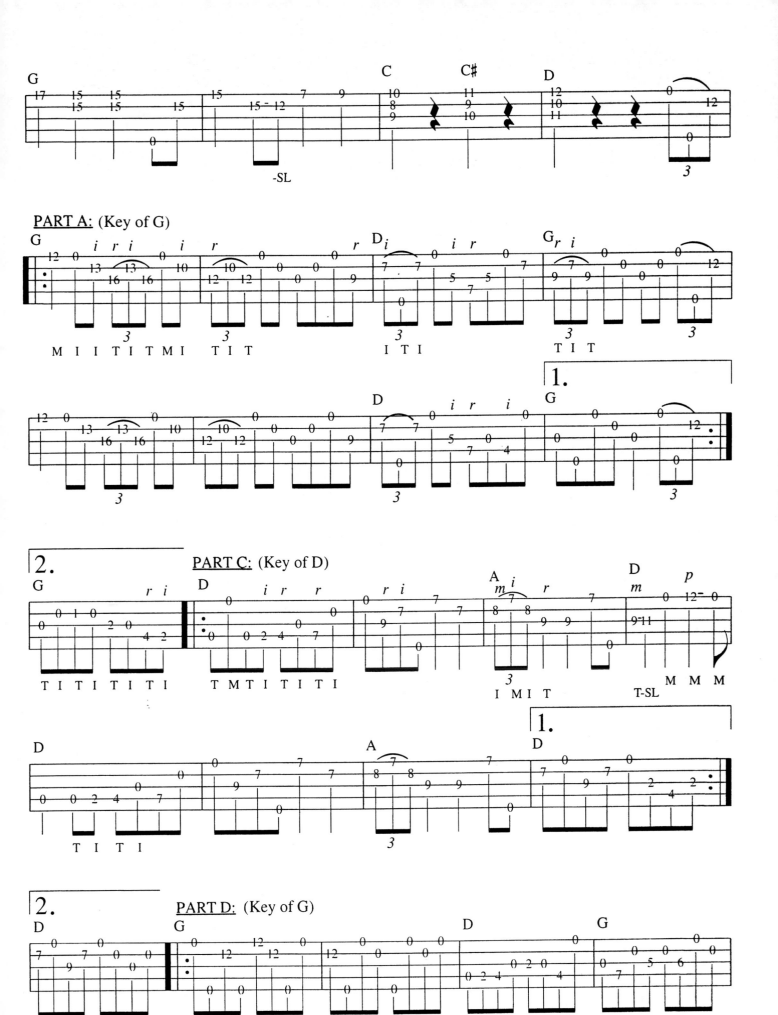

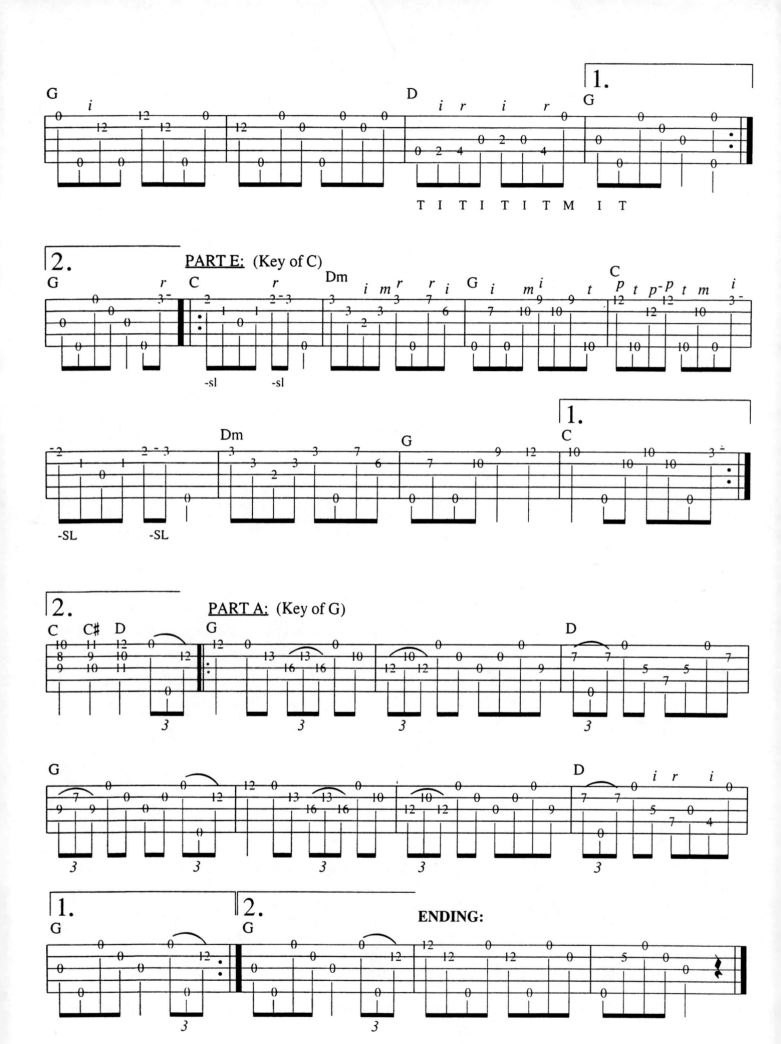

This well-known fiddle tune is a favorite among banjo players. Following are three different arrangements. The first arrangement (below) is a very standard way to play this tune. You can go directly into the subsequent arrangements without a break, or another instrument can take a break in between.

This tune is usually played in the key of A (place the capo on the 2nd fret).

Gray Eagle
Variation 1

- *Part A uses melodic-style licks.*
- *Part B primarily uses rolls, while holding partial chord positions.*
- *Hold the G chord (F position) for the final G chord in Part B.*

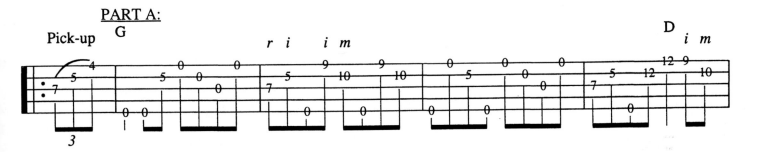

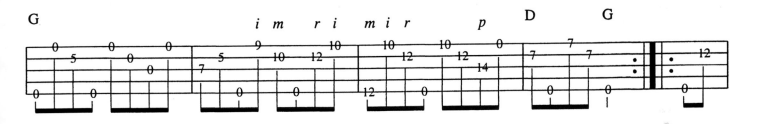

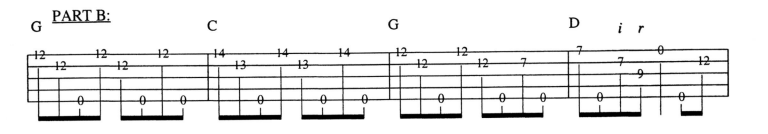

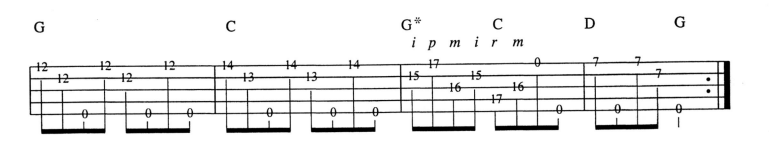

This variation is often played as a second variation. Notice that the scale line travels up the neck in Part A. Also notice that Part B employs harmonics or chimes at the 12th fret.

Gray Eagle
Variation 2

• *Using harmonics in Part B.*

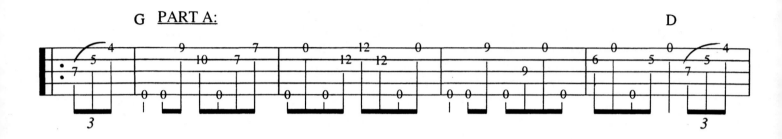

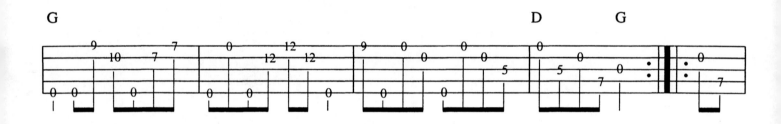

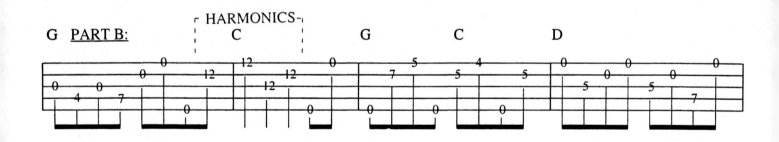

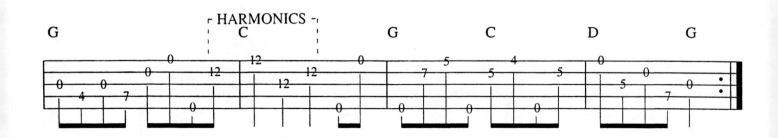

This variation is slightly more advanced than the previous ones. Notice that Part A uses licks which are based upon the chromatic scale as well as on the diatonic scale. However, Part B is the standard way to play the final variation to this tune. People often play Part A of variation 1 with Part B of variation 3 (below) in order to play a more straightforward melodic-style third variation without the more complicated chromatic licks.

Gray Eagle
Variation 3

- *Using chromatic licks in Part A.*
- *Playing a standard last variation for Part B.*

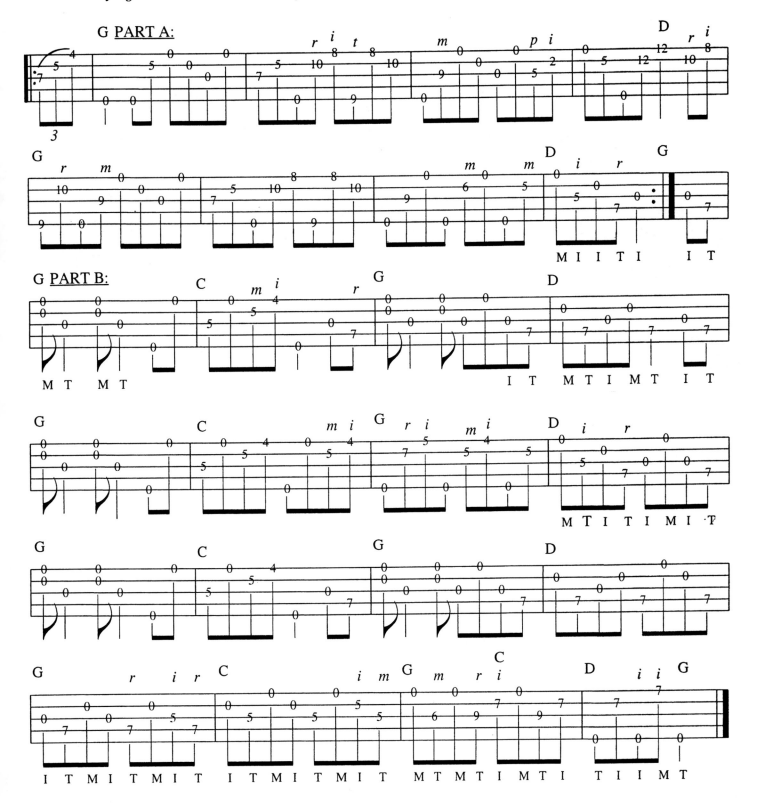

USING
CHROMATIC LICKS

The following songs demonstrate the use of licks which are drawn from sections of the *chromatic scale.** Although you can play an entire variation using chromatic licks for every chord, generally these licks are used only for a few bars in order to add a surge of energy and excitement to a song. Try to locate the chromatic licks in the second variations for "Hamilton County" and "Cumberland Gap" in the following pages.

The chromatic scale uses every tone along a single string of the banjo.

*The basic scale consists of 12 tones:

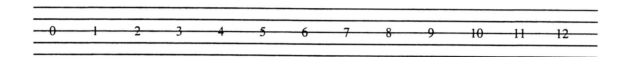

Chromatic licks extract eight-note sections from this scale and begin with a note which belongs to the chord for which the lick is being applied. Note: Many chromatic licks combine 2 measures (16 notes) in order to achieve the full effect.

G-CHORD LICK:

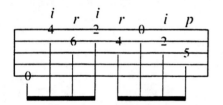 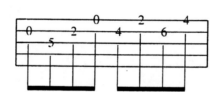 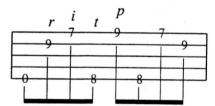

C-CHORD LICK:

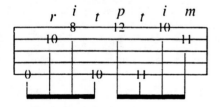 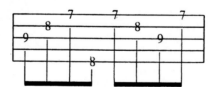 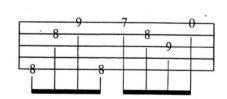

D-CHORD LICK:

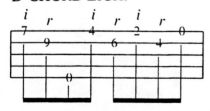 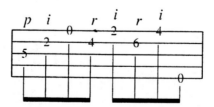

A-CHORD LICK:

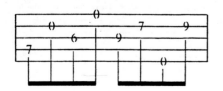 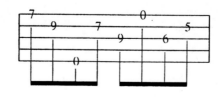

This is one of my favorite Berline & Munde tunes. After you have worked through this arrangement, try substituting different licks for some of the ones used here. For example, play the standard G lick for line 3, measure 3.* Also, play the D licks used for "Don't Let the Deal Go Down" in lines 4 and 8 for the D chord. Notice that the effect is entirely different.

Hamilton County Breakdown

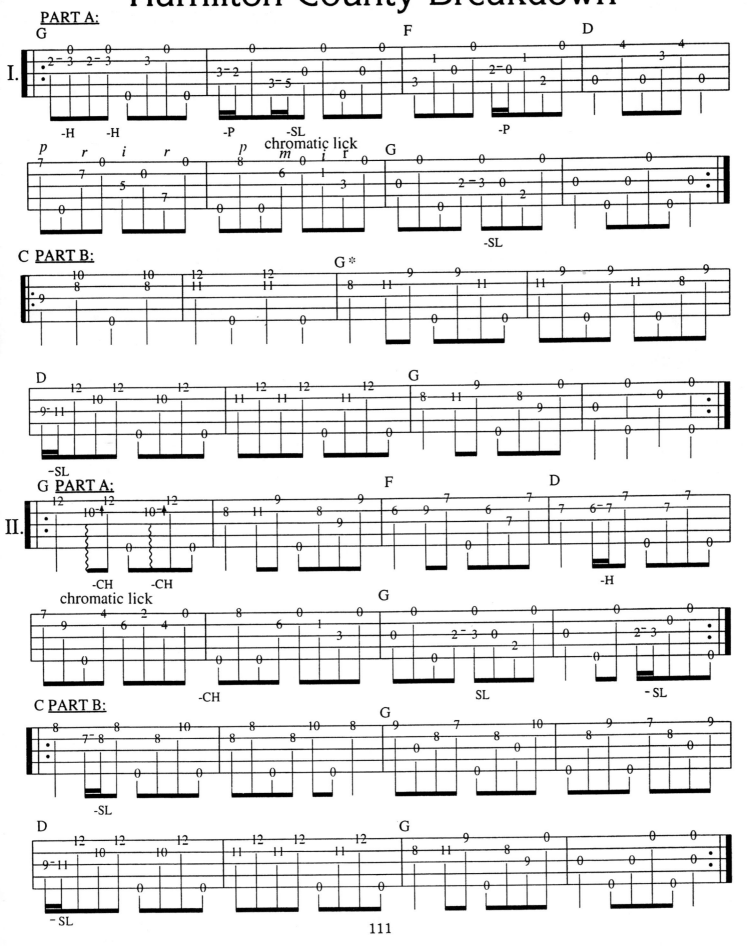

111

This arrangement uses chromatic licks (based upon the chromatic scale*). Notice that the left-hand fingering is indicated above the tablature. For practice, substitute Scruggs-style licks for the opening G chord and for the D chord in the 4th line, measures 1 and 2.

Also notice that the notes which are used for the D chord in the last line are the same ones we have used for the D chord throughout the book. However, in this lick, the rhythm is different. It can be fun to work with rhythmic variety in a standard lick, i.e., for ♫♫♫ play ♩ ♫♩. Both of these examples equal two beats using the same notes.

Hamilton County Breakdown

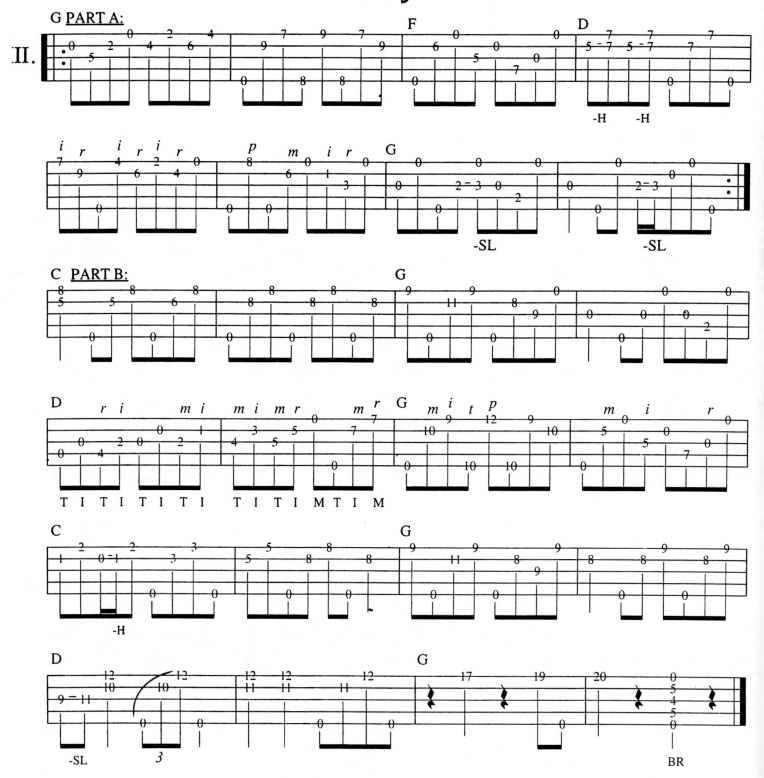

*Refer to *Splitting the Licks* by Janet Davis for more examples on the chromatic style.

A standard arrangement for "Cumberland Gap" can be found on page 22. Each arrangement below uses slightly different licks, which include chromatic tones to add extra motion to the overall effect.

Cumberland Gap

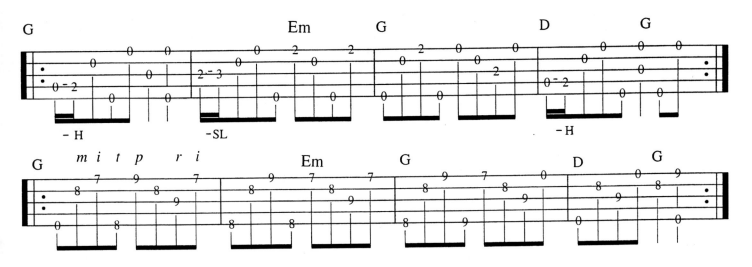

Cumberland Gap

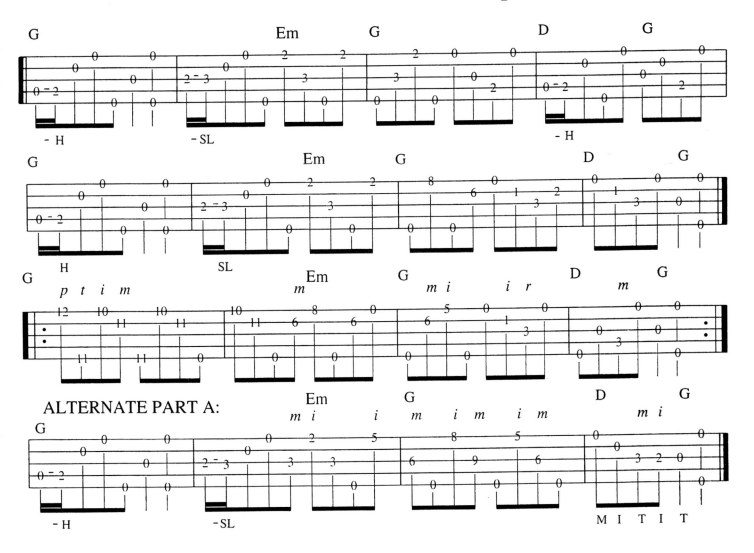

This arrangement for "Lonesome Road Blues" substitutes several advanced licks for the standard licks used for this tune on pages 44 and 59. It also travels the entire fingerboard, combining high pitches and low tones for contrast.

Lonesome Road Blues

- *Using advanced licks.*

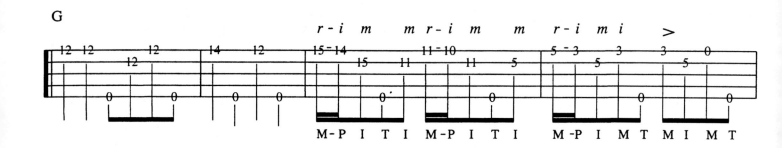

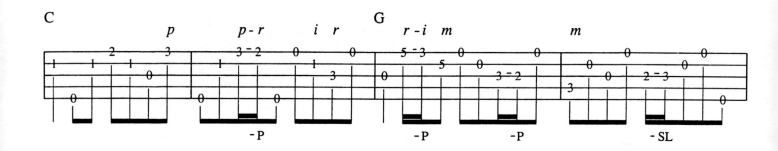

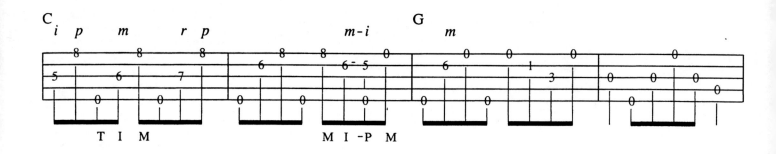

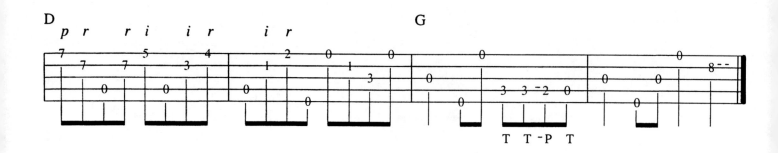

114

This is a traditional gospel tune that has been performed by many different bands. Bill Monroe and the Bluegrass Boys have recorded it several times. Also, The Seldom Scene has an excellent version of this tune. Compare the chord progression to the one used to play "Train 45." Notice that they are the same. However, the songs do not sound alike at all. One reason for this is the tempo used for each tune. "Train 45" is played at breakdown speed, while "Working on a Building" is played at a moderate tempo.

Working on a Building
Variation 1

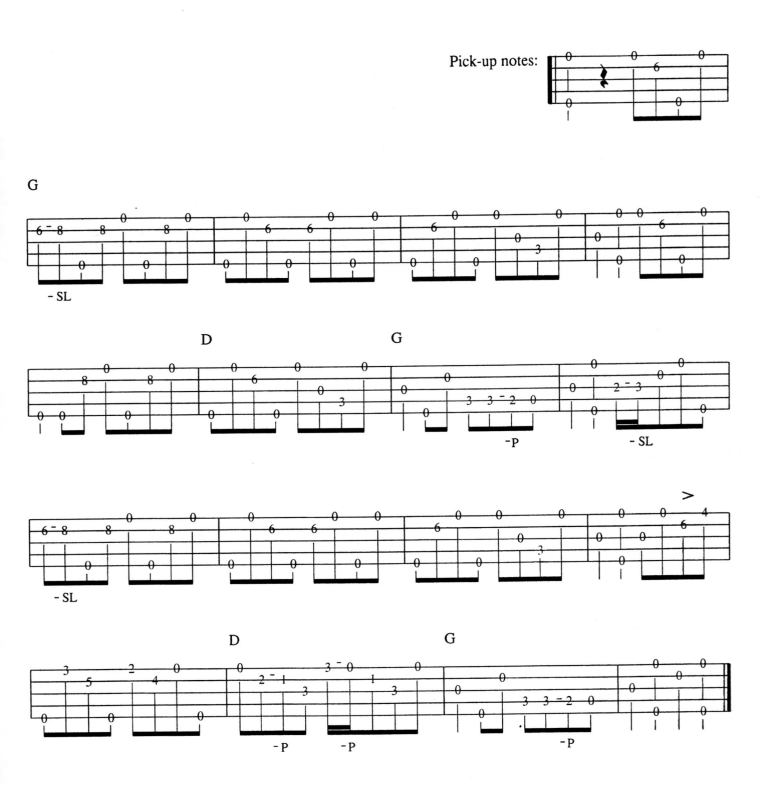

Working on a Building
Variation 2

- *Using chromatic-style up-the-neck licks.*
- *Using the same chromatic-style G lick (measures 9 and 10) used in "Lonesome Road Blues" (page 114, measures 3 and 4).*

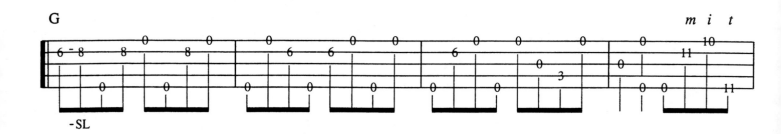

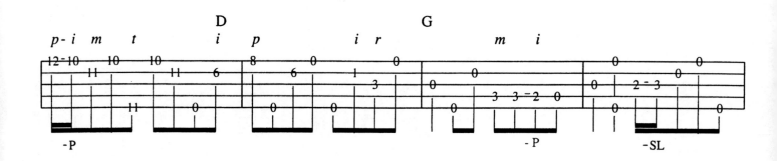

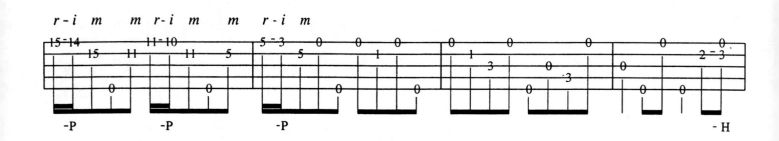

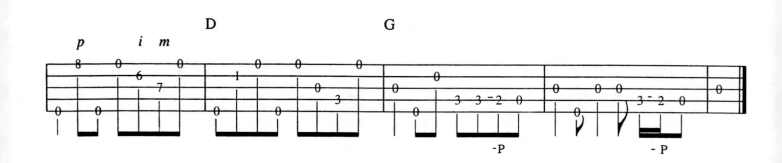

The single-string picking in Part A below is a standard way to play this tune. (Alternate the right thumb and index fingers.) Part B is played up the neck. Notice that the same lick patterns are used for both the G chord and the F chord. Notice also that the F-chord licks are played 2 frets lower than the G-chord licks. (Play any G lick 2 frets lower, and you have an F lick.)

Salt River

• *Capo on 2nd fret (key of A).*

Traditional

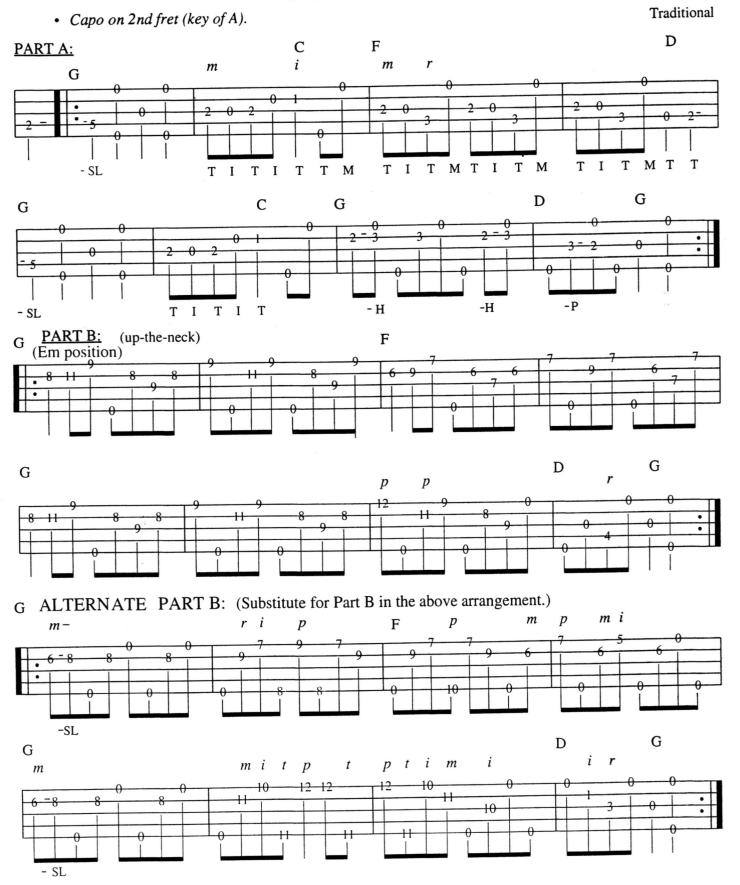

117

SINGLE-STRING LICKS

Single-string picking has become extremely popular in the 1990s . . . in the original Reno style, in the Adcock style (which retains the Reno flavor), and in the more jazz-like Fleck style of playing. Don Reno usually receives the credit for developing and popularizing single-string picking in the 1940s–1970s, while Eddie Adcock, Larry McNeeley, Bela Fleck, Scott Vestal, and other contemporary players have advanced this style of playing into new realms.

As with the melodic and chromatic styles, the single-string style uses scales to form the licks which are played for the chords of the song. However, the single-string style requires picking the same string several times in a row, rather than playing each note of the lick or scale on a different string. This style of picking causes the banjo to have a somewhat different timbre or tone quality which is very exciting and driving.

Generally, this style deviates (often greatly) from the basic tune or melody of the song, although it can also be used to play the basic tune (e.g., "Dill Pickle Rag," page 122). Although an entire variation can be played using the single-string technique, more commonly, single-string licks are combined with more traditional licks or with melodic or chromatic licks. (Bela Fleck uses a variety of styles in a single arrangement: Scruggs, melodic, chromatic, single-string, and even a frailing style.)

Technically, the single-string style of playing involves a strong, active left hand which frets the scale tones, while the right hand alternates picking the string(s) with the thumb and index finger. Most of the single-string licks are moveable fingerboard patterns which are based upon playing scales, and involve picking the same string several times in a row. However, it is also helpful to realize when learning to use these patterns that the left-hand positions for most of the single-string licks correspond to a chord position (D, F, or barre position) for the chord being played. In other words, many G-chord single-string licks are played in the same fingerboard area as the chord positions for the G chord. To play the same patterns for the C chord, you will move to the corresponding C-chord position to begin the pattern.

The following licks are fairly common single-string licks which can be used for any chord, depending upon where the pattern is played on the fingerboard. Notice that the left-hand fingering appears above each pattern.*

NOTES_____

*1. Many people barre their left index finger across the strings at the lower fret number of the corresponding chord position and hold it as an anchor, while moving only the middle, ring, and pinky when required to play the other notes in the pattern. This is not possible for all single-string licks, but often works well with licks which work from the *D position* and *F position* for the chord. This is only a suggestion, however, and not a requirement to play the licks.

2. The right hand should usually be placed in the Y position on the head for the up-the-neck licks. The music will sound better and the single-string licks should be easier to play from this position.

MOVEABLE LICKS
FINGERBOARD PATTERNS

D-POSITION LICKS (Note the relationship of these licks to the D position for each chord):

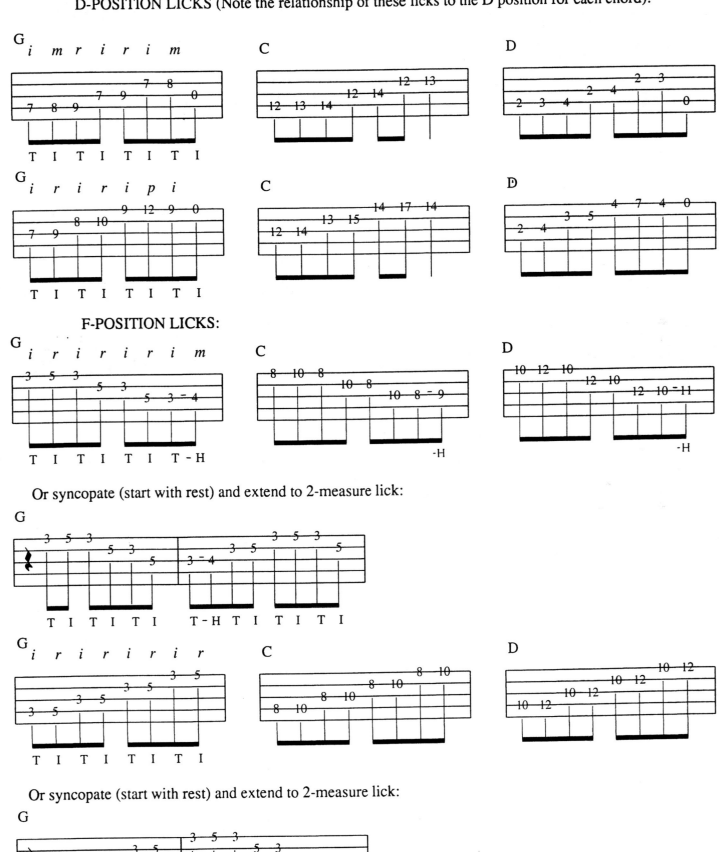

F-POSITION LICKS:

Or syncopate (start with rest) and extend to 2-measure lick:

Or syncopate (start with rest) and extend to 2-measure lick:

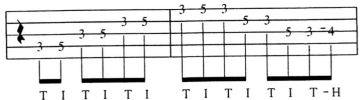

F-POSITION LICKS CONTINUED (All G-chord licks can also be played 12 frets higher):

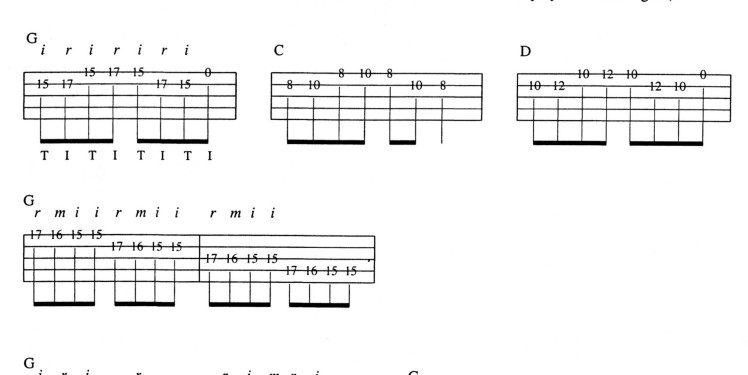

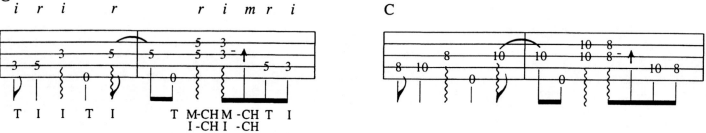

BARRE-POSITION LICKS:

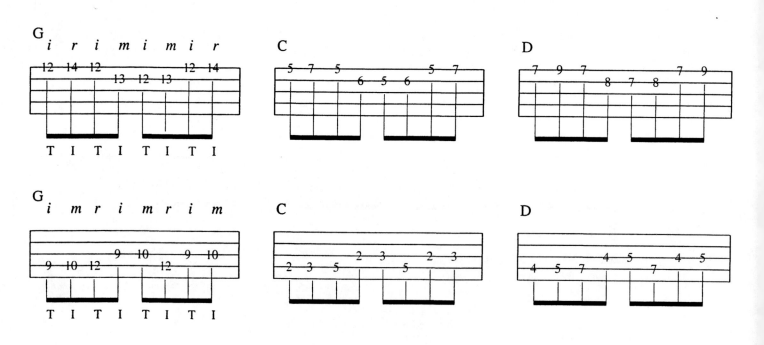

"She'll Be Coming Around the Mountain" uses the same chord progression that is used to play "Red River Valley" and "Mama Don't Allow." Although the same licks can be used for all three of these songs (the same arrangement), each tune will easily be identifiable if the melody is included. Notice that the positions of the chords being played are determined by where the melody notes fall. In other words, the chord position is chosen so that it includes the fret number playing the melody note.

She'll Be Coming Around the Mountain

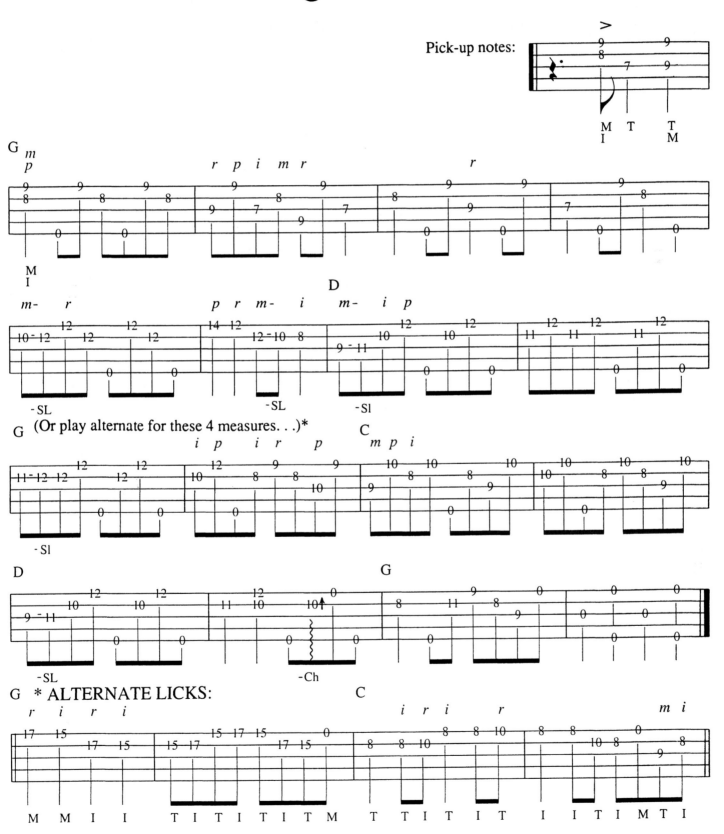

121

This is a popular fiddle tune which is a lot of fun to play. The arrangement below uses the forward roll pattern as the basic right-hand roll, while the left hand holds a 6th-chord position pattern for each chord. Notice that the forward roll is excellent for achieving the ragtime effect on the banjo.

The single-string work for this tune stays with the basic melody, and is used primarily when open strings are played. Notice that this arrangement does not use licks which deviate from the basic melody. (Single-string picking can be used either way — to play the melody, or deviate from it.)

Dill Pickle Rag

- *Using single strings to pick the basic melody in the down-the-neck area.*
- *Using the forward roll as the primary roll pattern.*
- *Holding 6th chords with the left hand for the roll patterns.*

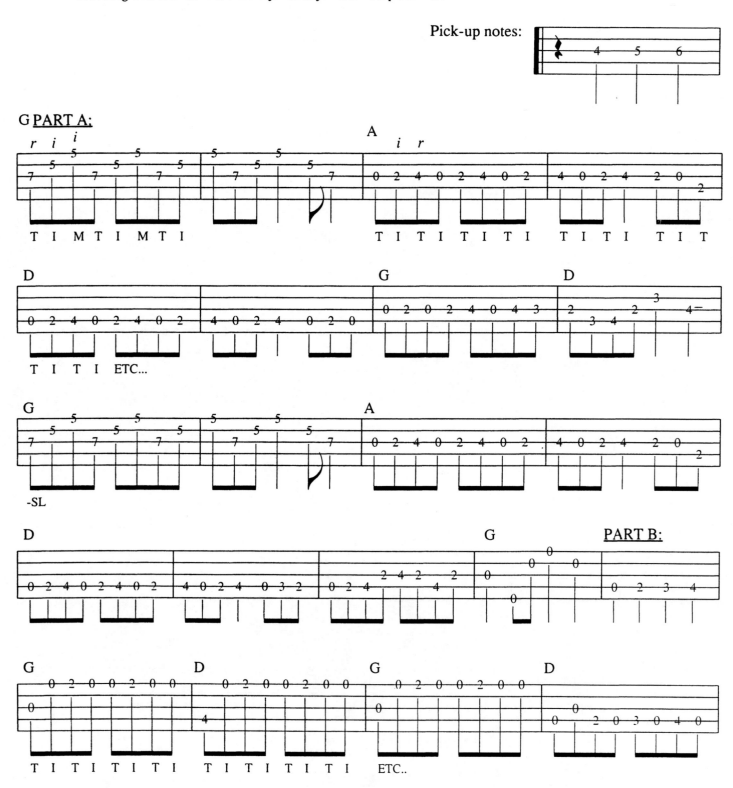

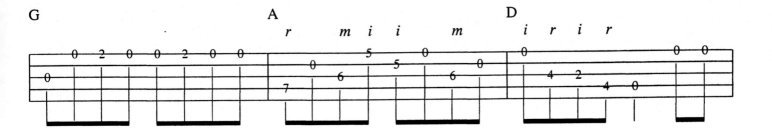

PART A:

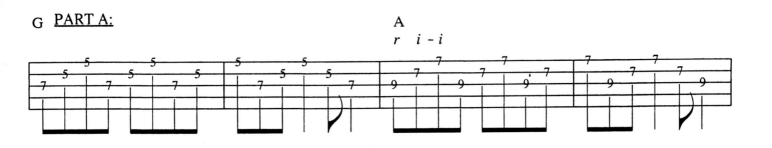

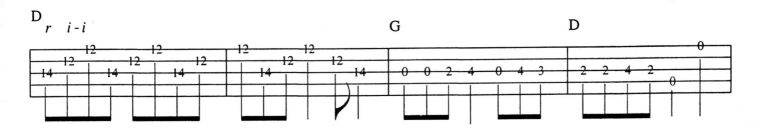

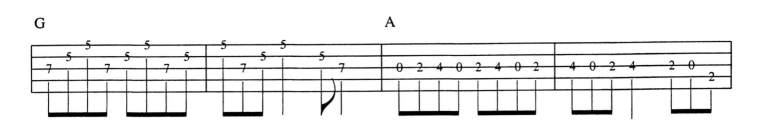

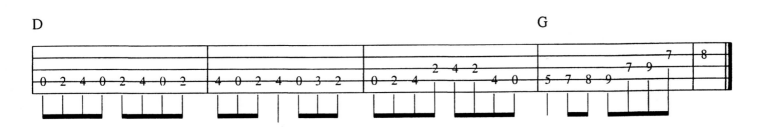

This is a well-known tune which is played by many fiddlers. The arrangement below is patterned after the style of Don Reno. Notice that it uses the forward roll as the basic roll pattern while the left hand holds the indicated chord positions. This is a commonly played roll for ragtime songs. A single-string lick is played for the C chord as a "fill."

The substitute licks presented on the next page can be used to create additional arrangements.

Black and White Rag

- *Using a single-string lick for the C chords as a fill-in lick.*
- *Using the forward roll as the basic roll pattern.*

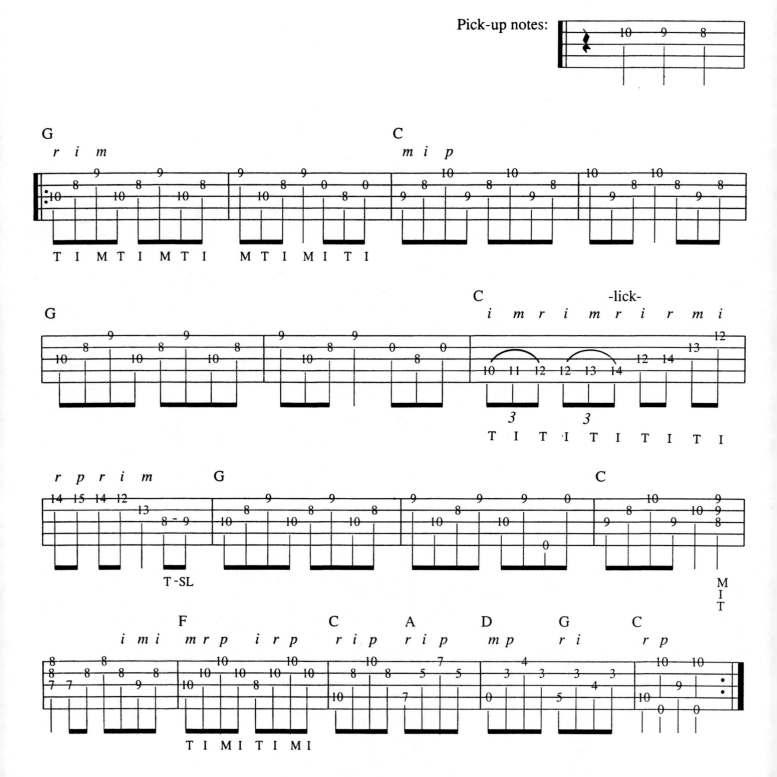

BLACK AND WHITE RAG — ALTERNATE LICKS

Each of these licks can be substituted for the corresponding chord(s) in the arrangement on the previous page. The licks are interchangeable.

ALTERNATE LICKS:

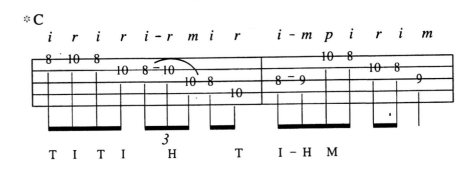

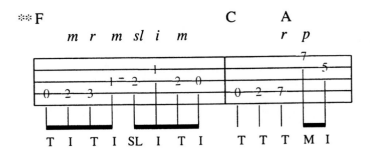

Ending: Substitute the first measure below for the last measure of the arrangement on the previous page, then follow with the ending.

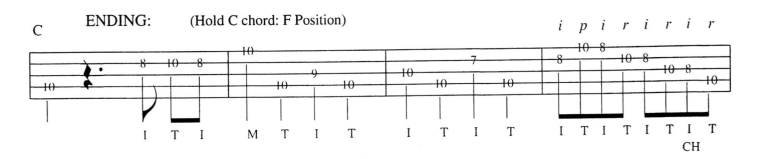

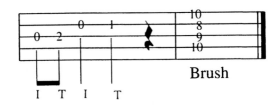

Brush

This arrangement uses a single-string pattern for each chord. For fun, substitute the alternate licks for the D chord to create different arrangements.

Salty Dog Blues

- *Using single-string licks for each chord.*

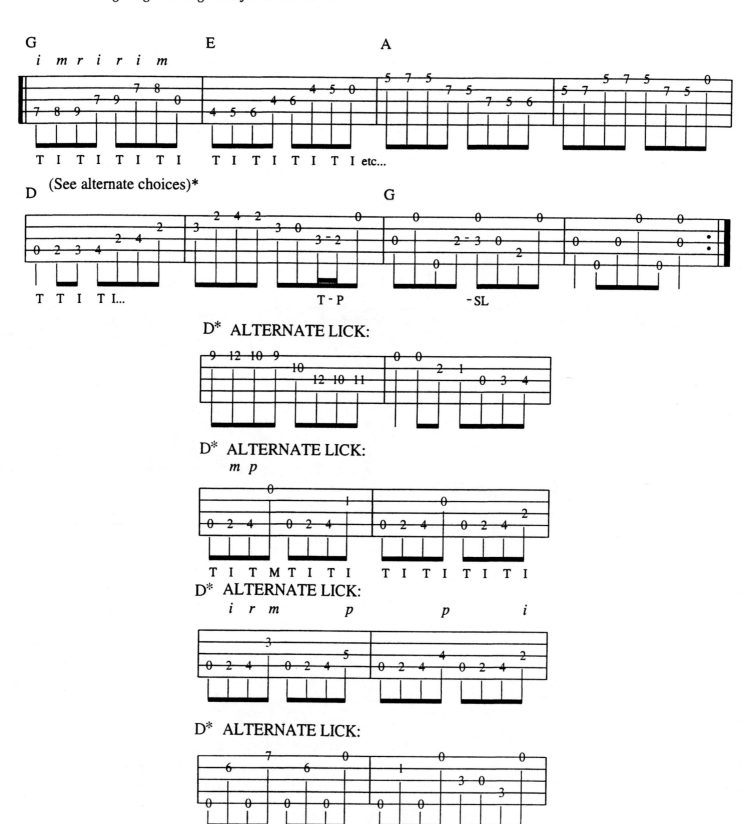

Play through Part A of this arrangement twice; then choose any Part B to follow it. (Part B should also be played twice.)

Salt River

- *Using a single-string lick for the F chord in Part A.*
- *Using standard Reno-style single-string licks for Part B.*

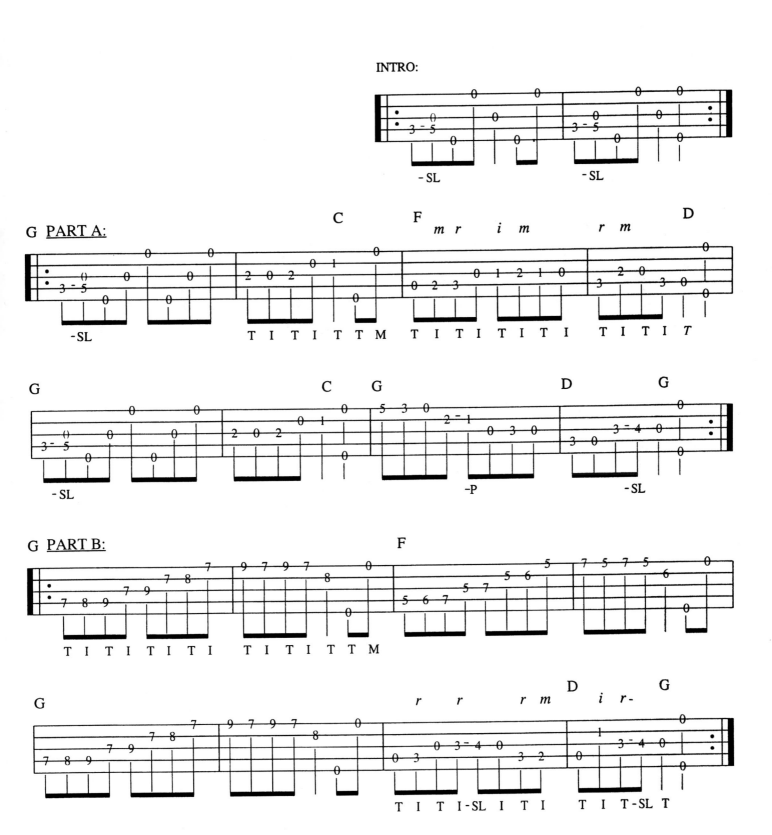

Each of the following can be played for Part B in the arrangement of "Salt River" on the previous page.

SALT RIVER — PART B
- *Using Fleck- and Vestal-style single-string licks for each chord.*

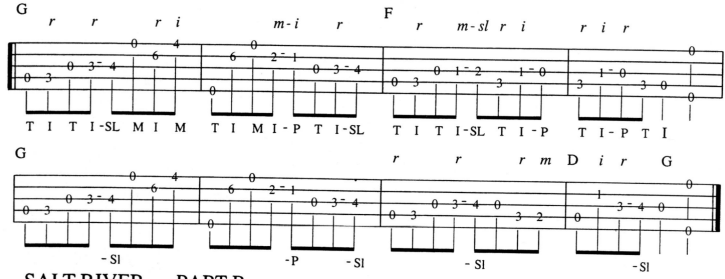

SALT RIVER — PART B
- *Combining single-string licks with chromatic-style licks.*
- *Notice the chromatic scale in the first 4 measures.*

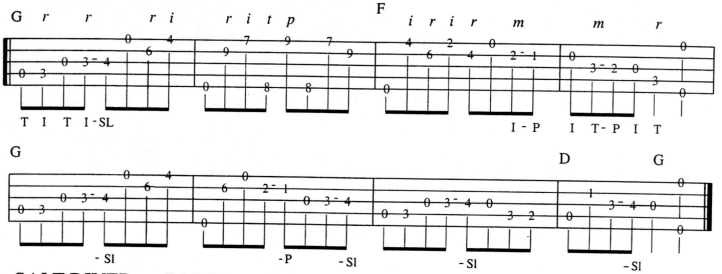

SALT RIVER — PART B
- *Using single-string picking instead of the chromatic-style to play chromatic licks.*

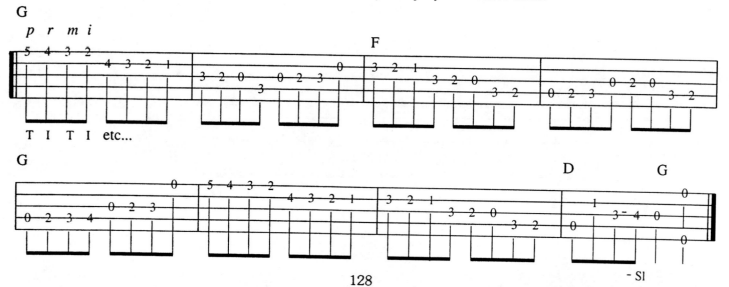

USING BACK-UP LICKS
FOR UP-THE-NECK LEAD ARRANGEMENTS

It is not uncommon to play *back-up licks* when playing a *lead break* for a song in the up-the-neck area. Back-up licks are moveable patterns which can be played for any chord, and for this reason are easy to adapt to any song. When back-up licks are used in this manner, they are usually used for songs which are played at a moderate to slow tempo. As you will see with the following songs, back-up licks can be used to provide certain effects, e.g., a bluesy effect; a bright and bouncy effect.

INTERCHANGEABLE BACK-UP LICKS:

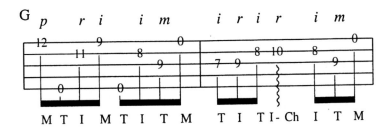

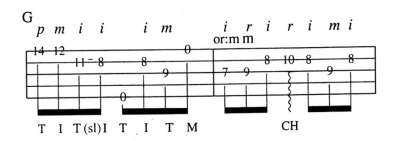

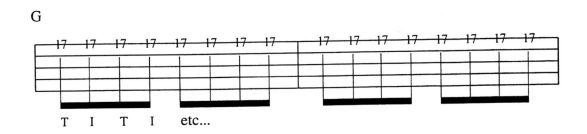

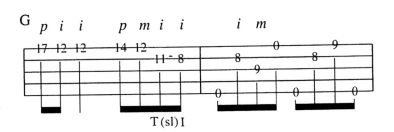

Note: For more on back-up, see *Back-Up Banjo* by Janet Davis (a Mel Bay publication; 238 pages of licks, information, and songs, plus a 90-minute tape).

The following chord progression has been played for several different songs. Among them are "Banjo Boogie," "Heavy Traffic Ahead," and "Foggy Mountain Special." Many of the licks used for this arrangement also serve as effective back-up licks. Note: Throughout this arrangement you have a choice of using the open fifth string or the second string at the 8th fret. (Both play the same tone — G.)

12-Bar Blues

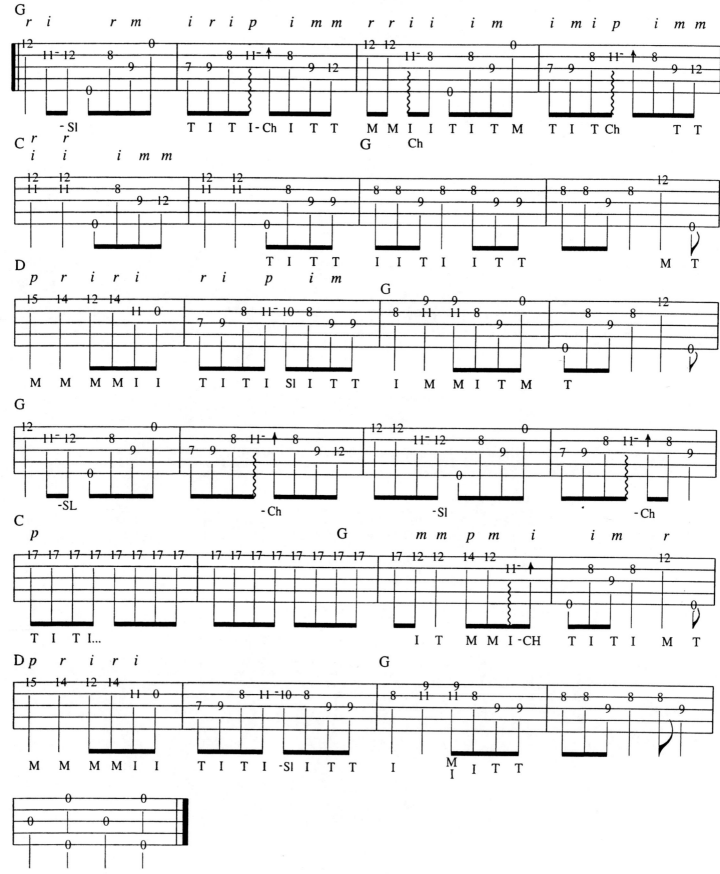

This is another traditional gospel favorite. The first arrangement below establishes the tune for the song. Each of the up-the-neck arrangements begins with the same lick but will then substitute different licks within the body of the arrangement. Notice that this tune uses the same chord progression that was used for "Working on a Building." However, the two songs come across as entirely different songs. Even though the tempo is similar, the types of licks that are used for each tune are quite different and result in an entirely different effect.

Hear Jerusalem Moan

Variation 1

- *Basic variation establishing the melody.*
- *Uses an extra fill-in lick at the end between verses.*

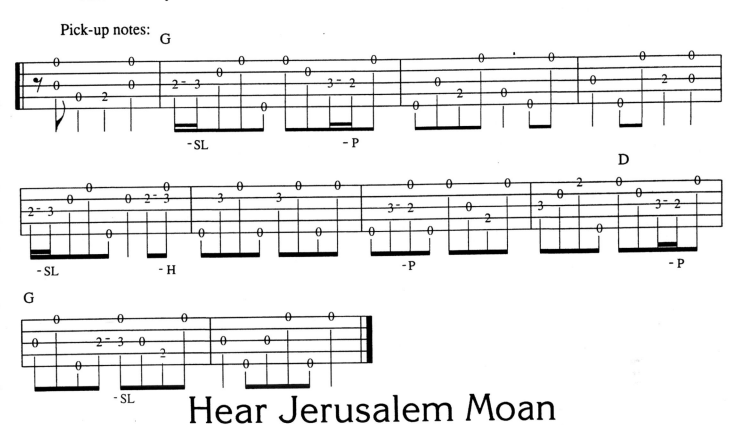

Hear Jerusalem Moan

Variation 2

- *Using back-up licks in measures 1, 2, and 6.*

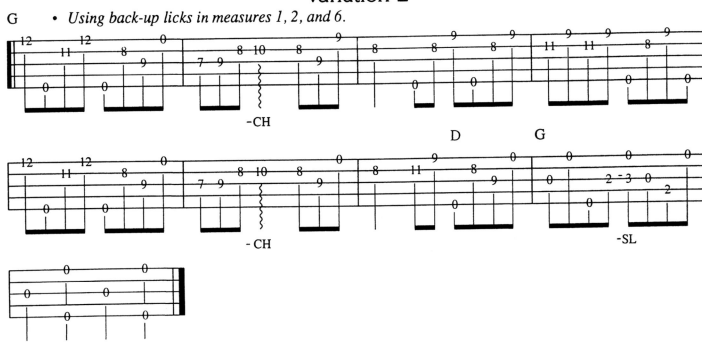

Hear Jerusalem Moan
Variation 3

- *Using back-up licks in measures 1, 2, 5, and 6.*
- *Includes melody in measure 3.*

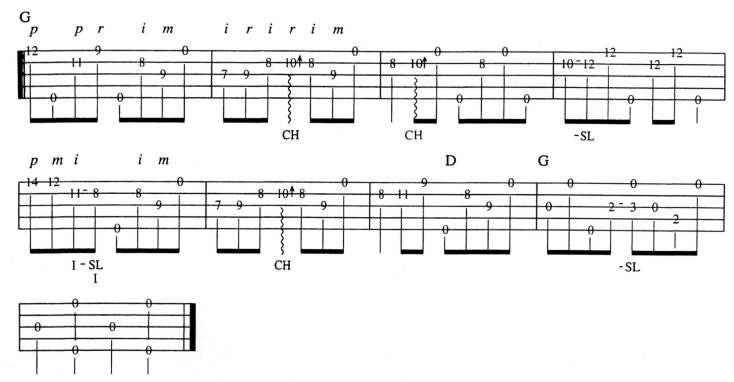

Hear Jerusalem Moan
Variation 4

- *Using back-up licks in measures 1, 2, 5, 6, and 7.*
- *Includes melody in measure 3.*

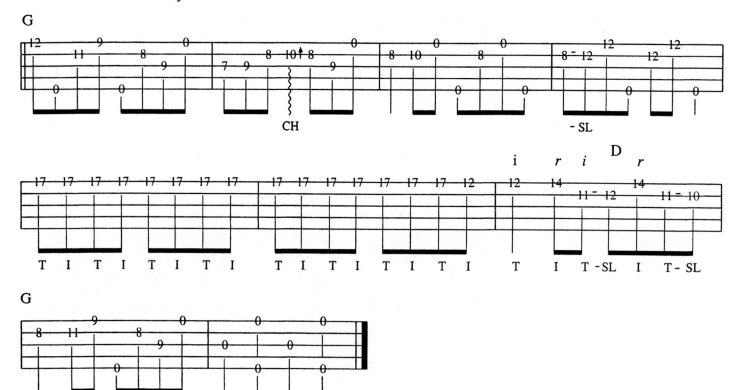

The following arrangement involves picking the same string twice in succession, using the same finger. This is played in a style that has often been used for back-up of songs played at a moderate tempo. Notice the bounce that is caused by the single-string technique. Earl Scruggs and Sonny Osborne can be heard playing in this style on many tunes. This is a picking style that is primarily played up the neck.

I Don't Love Nobody

SUMMARY
IMPROVISING

It is important to realize that keeping the proper time with the right hand and working from the proper chord positions, or with tones or fret numbers which will work for the song being played, will result in an effective arrangement, regardless of which licks are played. Experiment with different licks in these arrangements and try using different ideas to develop your own arrangements.

Also, remember to emphasize strongly specific notes within your arrangement. These can be melody notes, color tones, notes falling on a specific beat in the measure, or any note or notes that sound the best to your ear and feel the best to your fingers. This is one way a person develops his or her own style of playing. If you work within the context of the roll patterns and the bluegrass licks, you will achieve a solid bluegrass sound.

Note: For additional chromatic and melodic licks, see the advanced sections in my book *Splitting the Licks* (Mel Bay Publications).

Also, *The Major Scales* is a recommended book which is concerned with working in all areas of the fingerboard of the banjo.

ENDING A SONG

Each of the following can be played at the end of a song to provide a feeling of finality. (A good, solid ending will usually draw applause from an audience, even if the middle of the song had its problems.)

Endings: Group I

- *Substitute each example for the final D chord to end an arrangement.*
- *Each ending below is interchangeable.*
- *The right hand should be in the Y position for the last 2 measures when playing each ending below (right next to the fingerboard!).*

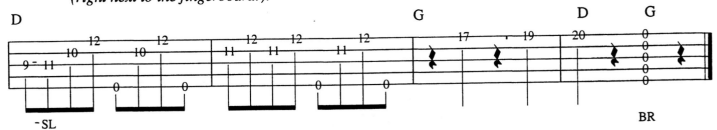

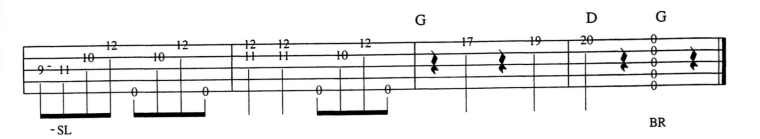

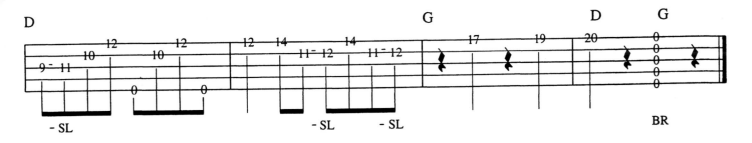

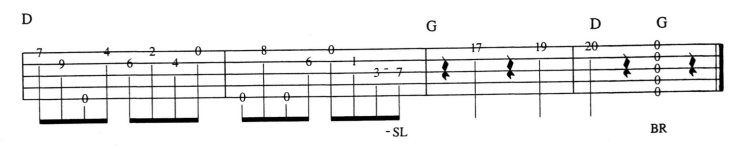

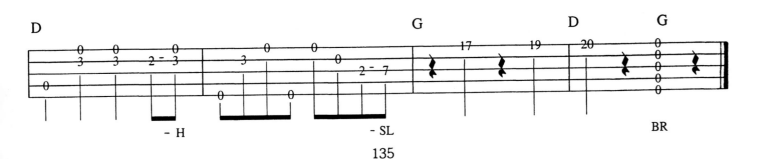

Endings Continued

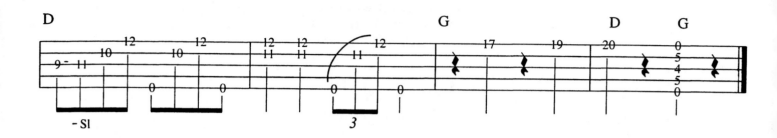

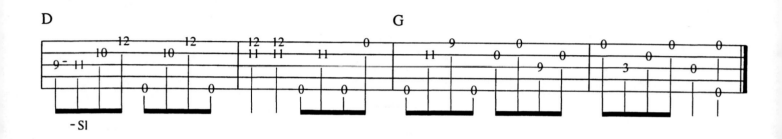

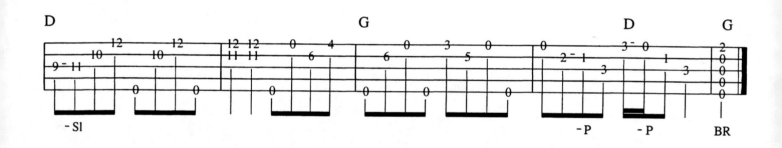

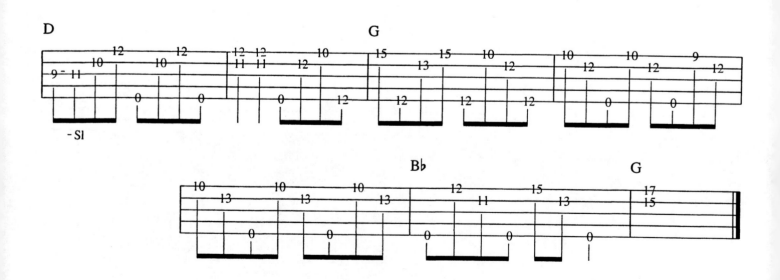

Endings: Group II

- *Substitute each of the following for the final G chord of any arrangement. These may also be substituted for the last 2 measures of any ending in Group I. (These endings immediately follow the final D chord in a song.)*

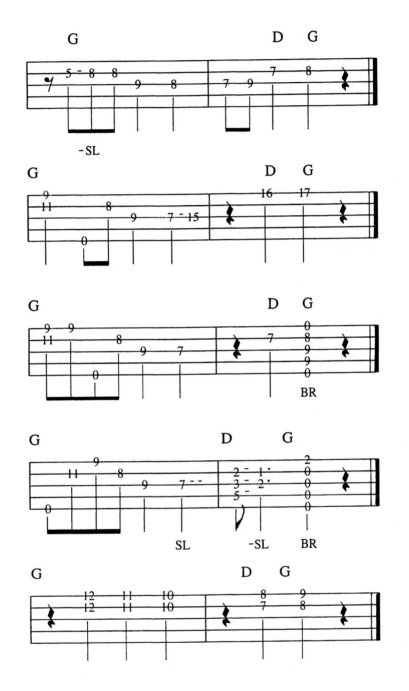

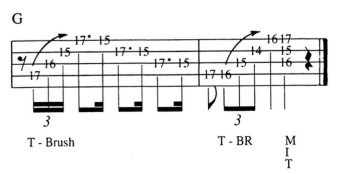

T - Brush   T - BR M
               I
               T

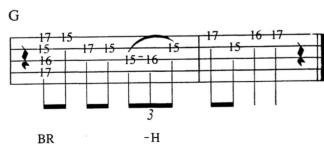

BR   -H

MOVEABLE CHORD-POSITION CHART
MAJOR CHORDS

The number by each individual diagram tells you on which fret the chord starts. Use the correct left-hand fingering to form each chord position (I = index; M = middle; R = ring; P = pinky).

BARRE POSITION

1 G	12 G
1 G# Ab	13 G# Ab
2 A	14 A
3 A# Bb	15 A# Bb
4 B	16 B
5 C	17 C
6 C# Db	18 C# Db
7 D	19 D
8 D# Eb	20 D# Eb
9 E	21 E
10 F	22 F
11 F# Gb	

F POSITION

1 F	13 F
2 F# Gb	14 F# Gb
3 G	15 G
4 G# Ab	16 G# Ab
5 A	17 A
6 A# Bb	18 A# Bb
7 B	19 B
8 C	20 C
9 C# Db	
10 D	
11 D# Eb	
12 E	

D POSITION

2 D	14 D
3 D# Eb	15 D# Eb
4 E	16 E
5 F	17 F
6 F# Gb	18 F# Gb
7 G	19 G
8 G# Ab	20 G# Ab
9 A	
10 A# Bb	
11 B	
12 C	
13 C# Db	

CHORD CHART — G TUNING
MAJOR CHORDS

Major chords are formed from the 1st, 3rd, and 5th tones of the major scale of the chord name.
There are three left-hand positions for all of the major chords.

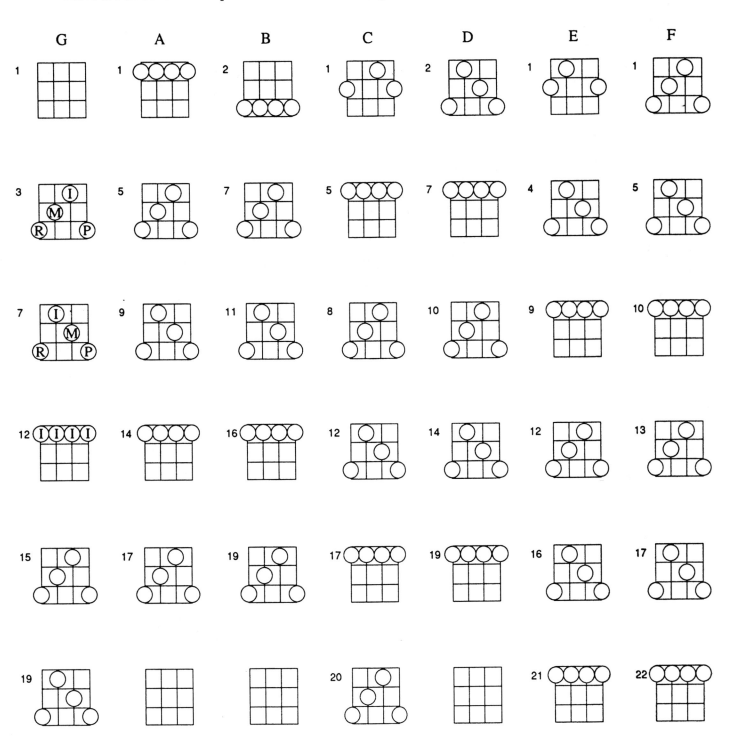

The number by each individual diagram tells you on which fret the chord starts.

MINOR CHORDS
(Symbol = "m")

A minor chord is formed by flatting the 3rd of the major chord of the same name. There are three left-hand positions for all of the minor chords.

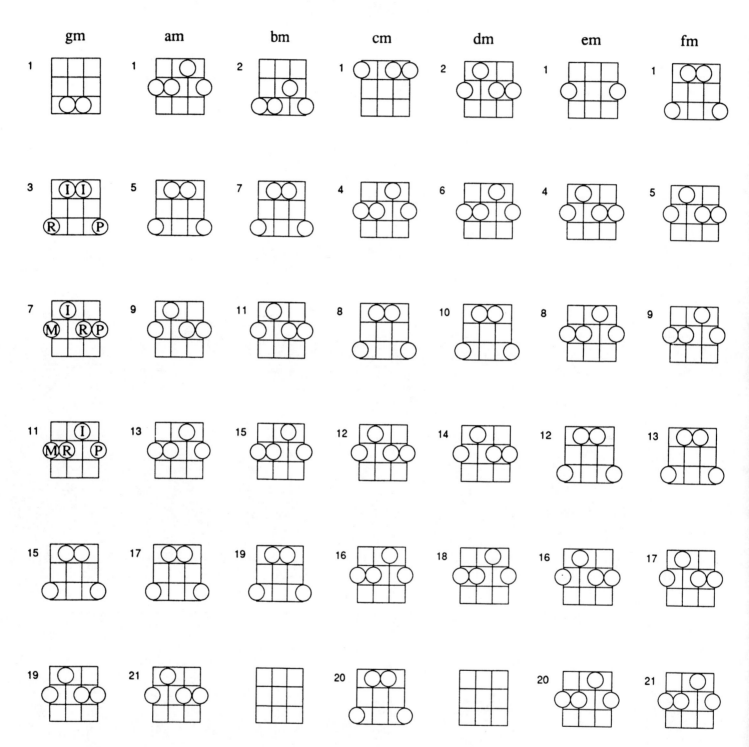

The number by each individual diagram tells you on which fret the chord starts. (Minor chords are usually indicated with small letters.)

DIMINISHED CHORDS
(Symbol = "○")

The diminished chord is formed by flatting the 3rd and the 5th of the major chord. Although the diminished chord can be formed by the left hand in several different positions, more commonly the ♭7th is added to the chord so that the same fingering position on the banjo can be used to play several diminished chords of different names. The following are the most popular diminished chord positions. (Each position can be played 3 frets higher for the same chords.)

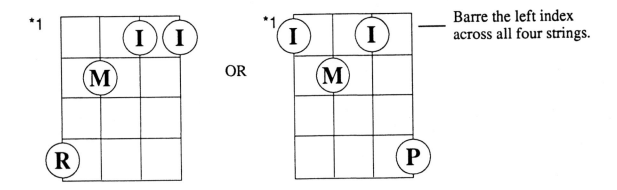

_____ Barre the left index across all four strings.

*When the lowest tones of these positions are held on the 1st fret, the chord is F♯°, A°, C°, E♭°, G♭°, and D♯° (*any* of these). The same position begun on any of the following frets will also result in the above chords: 4th, 7th, 10th, 13th, 16th, 19th.

When the lowest tones of these positions are held on the 2nd fret, the chord is G°, B♭°, D♭°, F♭°, E°, A♯°, and C♯°. The same position begun on any of the following frets will also result in the above chords: 5th, 8th, 11th, 14th, 17th, 20th.

When the lowest tones of these positions are held on the 3rd fret, the chord is G♯°, B°, D°, F°, A♭°, and C♭°. These chords can also be played at the 6th, 9th, 12th, 15th, 18th, and 21st frets.

AUGMENTED CHORDS
(Symbol = "+")

An augmented chord is formed by raising the 5th of the major chord of the same name. The left-hand fingering position is the *same* for all augmented chords.

The number by each individual diagram indicates the fret on which the chord starts.

DOMINANT SEVENTH CHORDS
(Symbol = "7")

A dominant 7th chord is formed by adding the flat 7th tone of the major scale of the chord name to the major chord.

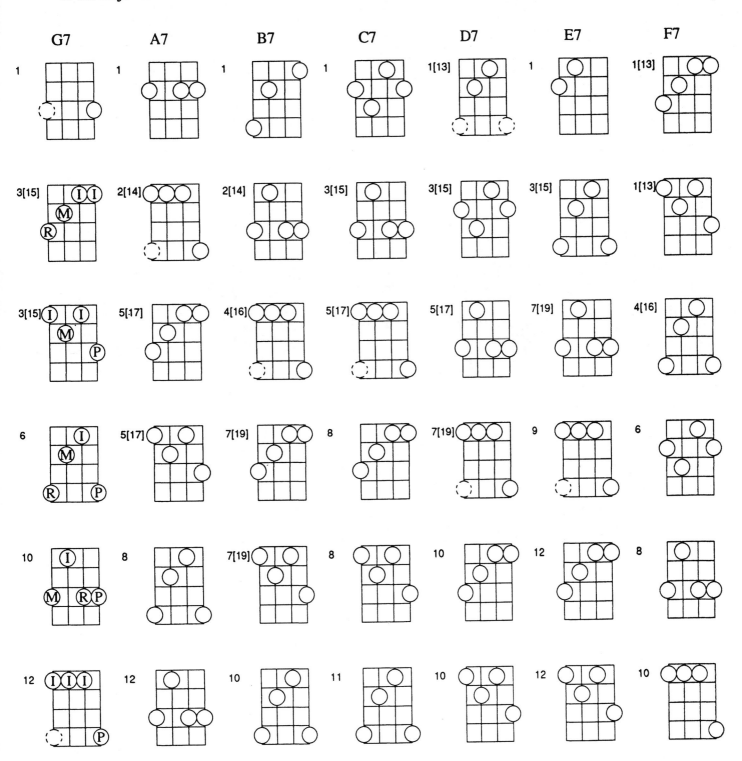

The number by each individual diagram indicates the fret on which the chord starts. (Two numbers by a diagram indicate two different locations.) ⊙ = optional.

Great Music at Your Fingertips